DO NOT REMOVE
CARDS FROM POCKET

Manny

a novel by

Isaac Rosen

BASKERVILLE
PUBLISHERS, INC.

Baskerville Publishers, Inc.
7616 LBJ Freeway, Suite 510
Dallas, TX 75251-1008

Library of Congress Cataloging-in-Publication Data

Rosen, Isaac
    Manny : a novel / by Isaac Rosen.
       p. cm.
     ISBN 1-880909-52-9
     I. Title.
   PS3568.0766M36 1996
   813'.54--DC20   96-42294

Manufactured in the United States of America
First printing, 1996

To my father, mother, Cynthia, Hale and Reed

On a July day in 1983, when it was hotter outside my body than inside, I became the first Jewish runaway in the history of New York City, maybe the world. Lying in bed, staring at the glow-in-the-dark plastic stars that my genius uncle had given to me, and which we'd pasted on my ceiling when I was seven, I fully expected another day of misery, the same old thing. I didn't think about running away. Didn't have the guts. Besides, Jews don't run away, right? That's something Christians do. Jewish kids might disappear for a few hours, but they come back when their stomachs start cramping with hunger or when they're convinced that Daddy is so freaked out by the missing bubola that he'll cave in and buy that skateboard the kid's been screaming for.

But my family, we weren't your textbook Jews.

The heat got me up, a dirty, smelly cloud of heat that drifted into my room through the screen window and sat on me like a fat man. I kicked the sheets off, and that exercise made me sweat even more, and I could imagine the fat man laughing. The heat's your alarm clock in a New York City summer. You get used to the noise — the sirens, the car

1

horns, the car alarms, the hollering alcoholics who walk the streets alone and in packs. But when the fat man sits on you, when he turns your bed into a sticky, wet pool that is sex minus the pleasure, you get up in a hurry and wash yourself off.

I walked to the bathroom. Didn't have an erection. Unusual. I'd had one of those sex/horror dreams that start cropping up when you're sixteen. You know, the kind when you break a woman in half as soon as you enter her. She shatters. This time, I'd been following a naked woman down First Avenue. I ran up to her, all aroused, and when she turned around, I saw my mother. Even in my dreams I was smart enough, or sane enough, to lose that erection fast.

I didn't shave, and that would turn out to be a good decision. I was a hairy beast who hated the blade.

We lived on 60th Street, a three-bedroom. And because cleaning was the only thing my father did well, he cleaned all the time, dusting the backs of photographs, using a tweezers to scrape the grime off a mirror's edge, vacuuming the refrigerator coils once a day. David Lipkin. My father, a big, loud son of a bitch whom you wouldn't have tagged as a Jew. He'd grown up in Paterson, New Jersey, second kid of my Russian grandparents, owners of the best pharmacy in the city, where bowls of chicken soup were always for sale, in case the behind-the-counter powders didn't do the trick. The first kid was Uncle Saul, two years older than my father. The Genius. Saul was the type who jumped out of the womb speaking in complete sentences about neutrons and the speed of light. It wasn't that bad. But Saul, the story goes, did grow tired of children's books by the time he was six, saying to his mother, "Why don't they simply put more words on a page, so we can get more of the story?"

Saul was the first in the family to go to college. Became a scientist, always going on about how everything could be explained by DNA. I wonder if he knew the number he did on my father. What explanation would he give? All those family parties where the older brother would entertain with Bach cantatas on the violin, while Lipkin the Younger slapped wooden spoons on aluminum pots. All the teachers who had taught Saul, or been taught by him, and then wondered if my father had been dropped on his head as a baby. My father wasn't a stupid kid, just average, but Saul grabbed all of my grandparent's expectations. He was the new country, electricity, running water, skyscrapers. My father was a cold Russian winter and a smelly bear skin, diseases with no cures.

I'm not trying to forgive my father for being such a jerk, just give a little context to his failures and his obsession with cleaning. When my grandparents died, the money that Saul had been giving to them monthly passed on to my father, which he sank into a series of sinking businesses. The button store, where my father refused to separate buttons according to color, size, or material, and put them in narrow, metal urns that customers didn't have the patience to rifle through. The candy store, which he set up next to the best candy store on the upper east side. The antique store. My father defined an antique as anything with scratches. He didn't buy the nice pieces and resell them at twice the price. No, he picked up the free, broken bookshelves and dressers that folks put out on their stoops for the garbage guys. And when people laughed or walked out of the store empty-handed, David Lipkin accused them of having no sense of history.

My father was mopping the kitchen. He used an old

toothbrush to get at the corners and underneath the peeling tiles. My mother, sitting at the table, lifted her feet automatically whenever he mopped near her. She'd probably already had two vodkas. I think she started drinking when the candy store sank. Now that my father owned a liquor store, he kept the house supplied at wholesale. When I was younger, she would read books and try to make my father laugh. Now she stared at a TV screen and didn't say a word. I could have switched the channel, from news to static, and she would have done nothing or nodded, as though the change had been a smart one, something she would have gotten around to doing herself if she had the time.

My father, David Lipkin, started hitting me about when my mother, Sarah Lipkin, started to drink, about when the candy store, East Side Candy, sank and the competition next door broke down the separating wall to expand its own sweet, sweet palace.

"Morning, Mom." Her hair was neat. She wore a dress. Anybody looking at her might have said she was getting ready for a busy professional day. But instead of a coffee cup, there was a glass of vodka in her hand. And her eyes weren't bright with energy. A defeated lady. Any day she'd stop getting dressed and combing her hair. She'd die here. She was, in movie terms, fading to black.

"Hello, Sweetie." She raised her arm in a drunken salute. I used to think that when she did this she was inviting me to take her hand. But whenever I did, she seemed surprised, uncomfortable with this contact with the outside world, and would take it back. I hadn't touched her hand in a year.

"You want some breakfast?"

"Yeah. I'll have some cereal.

"I think we have some corn flakes." And she stood up, unsteadily, and may have thought about walking to the pantry. She put a hand on her lower back, as though that were the problem.

"I'll get it, ma." She sat down, as slowly as she had stood up. Sometimes our eyes would meet, and through the vodka I could see some hint of the hell her life had become. But the vodka lens was getting thicker, and though you want to see your mother, really see your mother and communicate with her, sometimes you have to turn her off, treat her like a stranger you can walk away from and not turn back.

"I'll get the corn flakes, ma. It's okay."

"Watch the goddamned floor!"

My father was 200 pounds and six-foot-one. That's what he was, a big guy. That's what he had, strength. You don't think of these things when it comes to Jews. Smarts, yes, but not size. So, here's this guy wearing a tiny apron that he'd bought for his wife 20 years earlier, and which he'd adopted because his life sucked and he needed to clean. Could have been funny. The toothbrush was nestled behind his ear like a pencil. Could have been hilarious. I lifted my left foot from the tacky tile and looked for a place to put it down, but the tiles were all so clean that only my father could figure out which ones were yet to be done, and which were drying. Down my foot came, on a chance, and I was lucky. David Lipkin returned to his mopping. He bent over to strain the mop and it crossed my mind to kick his head. I imagined his head spinning around so that the last thing he'd see would be his back, his ass, and, if the angle was right, my smile.

There were ashtrays everywhere in the apartment so that when my mother and I smoked we would always have a place to flick. We sat at the table watching the news, each of us using a different ashtray. I turned the volume up when my father started vacuuming the refrigerator coils. He slapped the back of my head because, I think, the vacuum cord had fallen out of the outlet. I had my father's height, but not his size. One of these days, I thought, I'm going to have his size, and I'll have the desire on my side. Isn't that what the sportscasters say? Which team wants it more?

I didn't think about running away that day any more than I did on other days. But I always carried a lot of cash around with me, just in case. Genius Uncle Saul would send me money every few months, sometimes $50, sometimes $100. I didn't know why he did this, if he was telling me to buy a stereo or just get away. We didn't talk. Our families didn't get together. Not for Thanksgiving or Passover. There hadn't been a funeral in a while, so I didn't know how my little cousins were getting along. Not that I cared about them or their good life.

The thing about New York in the summer is that people stink. Stink. You end up holding your breath a lot, particularly when you walk by the bums and the homeless, because the stench slaps you, takes your appetite away, or makes your stomach churn if you've just had a meal. It's not just the unwashed folks, though. When the nice-looking women pass, the perfume and the sweat mix to tickle your throat, and you don't want to laugh. And the businessmen in their suits, their arms wet from wiping their foreheads, they smell, too. It's the ambition, I think, the fever. They're the only ones who stink in winter, when the cold keeps everyone else's odor under wraps, under clothes, clinging to the body and not letting go.

You look up at the sun in the morning, and it's already busy with the smell-making heat. But it's only 7:30. The fat man is only going to get fatter in the next few hours.

I walked up to the high school on 67th Street, just to see who was there. During session, I'd been going less and less. I wasn't learning anything. And the teachers didn't expect me, or anyone else, to. If you got through a day without screaming at the teacher, or getting into a fight, or lighting up in class, you had a good day, educationally speaking. They saw us as thugs, and I guess we were. The rich kids and the smart kids went to the private schools. That left us, the ones who needed to be managed rather than taught.

The school would call the apartment when I didn't show up, and my mother would tell them to phone the liquor shop because my father was in charge of discipline. He'd whack me a couple times, more because he was embarrassed than because he thought I was missing out on something. It still amazes me that my father could have been embarrassed about anything. I would have thought that embarrassment would snowball to cover his entire life, and I didn't think he was prepared for that. It's too much to ask that someone be embarrassed about everything he does.

Jamal and some of his friends were playing basketball, pretending they were stars, each of them saying that at one time he'd dunked on some monster goon, and, boy, that had been as good as sex. Whenever a rich white guy walked by, a guy in a suit or a white-coated doctor on his way to the hospital, the boys would slow down their game and through the chain-link fence offer pot or coke. Sometimes a sucker would buy two bucks of garbage for ten bucks. The best was when a doctor bit.

I was pretty good at basketball, but I didn't like to play when it was hot out, when I'd get all sweaty and need to go back to the apartment and my mother for a shower. Blacks look good when they sweat, strong. White guys look like they're having a heart attack. I just said "hey" to Jamal and his friends, and turned west.

I first started going into nursing homes when I was 15, on a kick, to see if I could get in. There are all these buildings in New York that you want to see the insides of — apartment buildings, embassies, businesses. But unless you can prove you're expected to a doorman or elevator man, you ain't going nowhere. Nursing homes were perfect. You just had to smile and wave to the old folks sitting by the doorway or in the lobby, and whoever was standing there in charge assumed you weren't going to steal something or shoot the place up. When you're young, particularly when you're white, even a big and hairy white kid like me, you don't get the fear bubbling.

I'd enter, smiling and waving, and walk up to the front desk, and usually on a nearby wall, there was a sign announcing who the citizen of the week was, or who'd won bingo a billion times, or who'd just crocheted a master quilt. There was a name and a picture. "I'm here to see Mrs. So and So," I'd say, pointing to the sign and showing pride that she'd been an outstanding citizen or master crocheter. Who am I? A friend of the family. Of course, sometimes it wouldn't work, if the place kept a list of permitted guests, or if they called the kids of the person to ask if they knew me. But I got through in a few places. I'd go to the room and meet the person. Now, these were the outstanding citizens and master crocheters. They weren't crazy or drooling. At first, I'd tell them I was a friend of the family, just checking in, but they'd want to know what side of the family, Aunt Jeannie's or Uncle Nathan's, and, in no time, my lies were as obvious as a herd of cattle on the Queensborough Bridge. So who are you? I just like to meet new people, I'd say.

It was true, in a sense. I had only one friend from school, Billy, who was incredibly smart but was always stoned. My parents were nothing. I didn't have siblings, which was a blessing for the world. Maybe I did like to meet new people.

I made friends all over midtown. Sure, they were on their way out, running to heaven, but I enjoyed them. Sara, 82, at the Sunshine Rest Home on Lexington, was my first pal. Her kids had put her there after her husband died, and they couldn't, wouldn't, take her in. She spoke fluent Greek, ancient and modern. Her son caught me visiting her one day, and thought I was a con man out for her money, even though she didn't have any (her son didn't know that), and the asshole told me to get lost. She threatened to disinherit him, and he backed down. She died in 1988. Left me a Greek dictionary. Left her son some debts.

Grant, at a home on 86th Street, was a sharp guy, even though he sometimes moved my checker pieces during a game. He'd been in every war in the past three hundred years. "I got metal in me," he often said, patting a thigh or his stomach and thinking he could hear the tinny sound. He was a plumber and had outlived all his family and friends. No kids. He said that when everybody you know is dead, you get sad, then you get bored. I saw Grant die. He'd just finished telling me how one day he was fixing a leak in the Dakota, how this movie starlet had showed him her breasts and had tried to seduce him away from the toilet pipes to her own pipes. Then he shook. Then he stiffened. I heard his last breath. An exhale.

I went to as many funerals as I could. Sometimes there was just me and a distant cousin.

That morning I walked into the Mayflower Home, an awful place that hid its dirt with institution-gray carpeting. All over the walls were pastel drawings of puritan themes — hard work and sober living — and the first Thanksgiving. It was the type of cold atmosphere that a central factory distributes to businesses around the country named Mayflower. Mayflower Restaurant. Mayflower Plumbing. Mayflower Florist. They all get the same pictures.

All the attendants were black, and they didn't like the residents, who were all white and hated blacks and made no secret of it. All except Jane. She was kind to everyone. And of all my nursing home friends, Jane was more interested in talking about me than about herself, which, of course, made me more interested in talking about her, because I hated to talk about myself.

She'd been all over the world. Never wanted to get married. Then she met this Englishman adventurer who fell for her. She'd been a beauty, her pictures showed. Had a spirit that would have made a dead man's dick hard, made it big enough to smack the coffin ceiling. They traveled together for five years before they got hitched. He said that she meant the world to him, and she convinced herself that she loved him. He had a stroke somewhere in Southeast Asia, I think it was Java. And she spent ten years writing travel books and articles, and taking care of him, this lifeless blob. He died, finally. Then she traveled again. Until she had to stop. Something about her heart. Mayflower Home was her sister's idea. She didn't want Jane to live alone. And after a while, neither did Jane, whose closest friends either lived in far-away countries or were buried in faraway countries.

"Got a fag, Josh?" We used to sneak cigarettes in her room. Close the door and stick a towel at the base so the smoke wouldn't give us away. She was tiny, maybe four feet tall, and I don't know where she put all that smoke, but she drew a cigarette twice as far as I could.

"For my favorite citizen of the week? You know I do." Citizen of the Week. That's how we'd met.

"So what are you doing today? Boy, it's a hot one. Like Algiers or something."

"I just had to get out of the apartment."

"Dad cleaning again?" I nodded. "Maybe you should stay here for a while." She drew half the cigarette in, and as she exhaled she thought. She had a lot of time to think with all that smoke. "Why don't I call downstairs and see if I can get another mattress. I can say I want to exercise on it during the day, and I'll keep it in my room. You can sleep on it and sneak out every morning."

"I'll be all right. Thanks, though."

"You sure?"

"Yup."

"They got some nice mattresses."

"I'm okay."

"I get the message. You reading these days?"

"No."

"You told me you were gonna do some reading. Where's the list I gave you?"

"I got it."

"So why don't you use it?"

"I go to the library."

"I know you go there, but you don't read. It's like going

11

to the movie house and not watching the movie."

"Library's free, Jane." She laughed. Smoke everywhere.

She asked, as she always asked, if my father had been hitting me. And I said, as I always said, a little. She walked behind the imitation-leather chair where I was sitting and stroked my hair, exactly where my father had whacked me because I'd let the vacuum cord fall out of the outlet.

"You got to get away from that bastard. He's taken too much from you."

"Lyle ever hit you?"

"One time, and I hit him back. He fell over backwards and got a fire poker up the ass." I almost believed her.

I never got to tell Jane about my big adventure. I'd looked forward to telling her about Manny and Patrick Henry and Francis Gallagher, but her heart blew up. I think I was on I-95, driving in Manny's rented VW Rabbit when it happened.

I go to her grave every year and smoke a cigarette with her. A quiet cigarette with Jane in the cemetery.

Central Park is the only place in New York that doesn't smell bad in the summer. There are bums on the benches, yes, and they stink as bad as they do on the street, I know it, but there's so much room in the park that you can walk around them and not have to inhale the stench. And the trees, grass, and bushes absorb the odors, just like kidneys do with the body's poisons.

I walked to my favorite part, the ball fields, and even though it was only 11 a.m., the softball players were going at it, drinking beer, playing games, eating hot dogs for break-fast. There were four games going on at once, so you could walk around the periphery of the fields, listen as the sounds of one game were drowned out by those of another. A great sports experience, but different because the fans here, passers-by and tourists, don't have a pre-set allegiance to either team. You just clap when someone does something well. Or, you decide you like a particular team because of the color of a uniform or how crude a team is. And if you like crudeness.

These boys of summer take their game seriously, which they probably shouldn't. It's softball, not baseball. You shouldn't take seriously a sport where the only injuries are caused by clumsiness. If a pitch hits you in softball, you pretend that it hurt you and then you smile, grateful that you're not doing a sport that has some risk to it.

I took a seat on the bleachers to watch what seemed to be the best game, Shlomo's Shipping and Moving versus a company called Sound and Vision. The score was even, 6-6, and Shlomo's team was in the field. They were my team. I didn't have much of a Jewish identity, but when a Jewish team was playing, and Shlomo sounded Jewish to me, I rooted for them, knowing that some other people were probably cheering for the other side just because they were playing Jews. A sharp-hit ball to third, cleanly picked up, and the runner is thrown out at first. The Jews retire the side. Rah, Rah, Rah.

Shlomo's Shipping and Moving, like every softball team in New York, had its quiet, outstanding athlete (third base), a fat pitcher who saw himself as the leader, and a fat manager whom the players laughed at because he talked about softball as if there were some strategy to it, as if the manager needed to do anything but announce who was on deck.

A weak man in his fifties stepped to the plate. In all his

13

years at the company, he'd probably shipped and moved everything to everywhere, paintings to Westchester, cabinets to Staten Island, pianos to Queens. He swung at the first pitch, a classic mistake, and the ball dribbled pathetically to the pitcher, who cautiously threw it underhand to first base. The hitter didn't even run, and the manager told him to always run it out because you never know in softball. The batter frowned. He wanted to be as good in softball as he was in the office, tracking a shipment of manila folders to Jersey City or a cargo of wicker furniture to the small town of Hudson.

Behind the backstop, behind the battered batter, was a tall thin woman dressed in black, with hair dyed blond. But I don't want to get ahead of myself. You see a lot of people in New York, people you never expect to see again. I used to think, when I was riding on the bus and someone got off, that I'd never see them again. Or when someone got into a taxi that sped off down Park Avenue. Or a foreign family in a horse carriage in Central Park. I'll never see you again. I'll never know you.

She bought a hot dog and watched the game for a little while. I saw her finish the dog and throw the napkin in the garbage. I had no idea where she went or where she was going to go the next day or the next. "I'll never see you again."

Shlomo's team lost. The Jews were beaten by the high-tech Christians. The game was still tied in the last inning, with two outs, when a soft grounder was hit to our pitcher. He could have thrown it to first for the easy out, but the runner on third was going home, no force, and our fat guy wanted a dramatic finish, a play that would have sent the battle into extra innings, with the momentum on our side.

So he threw it home, over the catcher's head, over the backstop. It landed where the woman had been standing. The pitcher threw his mitt on the mound and sat down beside it. His teammates, on their way to the bench, didn't walk near him, the smelly pile of shit.

"So, you think this is an easy game, huh," the pro softball player says to me.

"Compared to baseball, yeah."

"Sure, compared to baseball. Is that all you're saying?"

"Yeah, boss. That's it."

"All right, then."

"I give you guys credit."

"You should. This ain't like checkers or nothin'."

"Now there's an easy game."

"Tell me about it. You get hurt at checkers, you're a real pussy."

I bought a hot dog, covered it with mustard, and ate it fast, the way Jane took in cigarettes. Felt sick afterwards. But those New York City hot dogs get cold fast, and a cold hot dog is about as appealing as a fly laying eggs on your open cut.

When I stepped onto Fifth Avenue, the sun hit my bare arms, and I burped out some hot dog gas.

If people drove like they walked in New York, the morgue and the hospitals would do even more of a gangbuster business. Arms and legs would spill out onto the street. Sometimes it looks like there is some order on the sidewalk, people walking downtown stay to one side, and those walking uptown to the other. But this isn't a rule, and even if it was, there isn't a cop in his right mind who'd want to be on that detail. He'd have to nab the uptown-kid who jumps to the left lane because the lady in front of him has to stop and tie her shoe. Or the downtown-headed businessman who takes the curb route, hurried because the meeting he's called for 9 a.m. can't wait fifteen minutes. Or the tourists. They walk sideways, move to the left, to the right, whenever a honey-nut odor or attractive window display calls them. If they're from England, they appreciate order and rules. The Queen farts at six, takes a dump at seven, teas at four. But their driving and walking patterns are all screwed up. So all the Brits who come to New York walk on the wrong side. If they see the problem and move to the other side of the side-walk, they do it too slowly. Can't win.

In the center of the sidewalk, God bless him, is the hand-out man. He has a stack of papers that tell you aspirin is on sale at the pharmacy down the street or a chicken dinner, including fries, can be had for a steal on the corner. You see him when you're ten feet away from him. He's short, but he has the power to screw up the walking pattern like no one else, even more than the Brits. Why? Because he uses his arms. He stretches them out, waving the pieces of paper, blocking four feet of sidewalk. Corks up the whole New York City bottle. Most city-folk try to ignore the hand-out man. But tourists, suddenly presented with a piece of paper, stop and inspect it. Suddenness is the best strategy for the hand-out man. He targets his customers, and into the groin of each of them he thrusts the bargain-announcing paper. As a defensive move, the passer-by covers his groin and ac-cepts the paper. The baton has been passed. Even the most hardened city-boy is sometimes forced to take the baton.

I never knew, still don't know, how the business that

hires the hand-out man can tell whether he's doing the job. He's not standing directly outside the shop, so the owner can't just watch. Your first thought on seeing the hand-out man is, why doesn't he toss the papers in the garbage, go get a cup of coffee, and return to the business empty-handed, saying he'd done his part, now where's the paycheck? So what does the boss do? Sends a lackey to check the nearby trash cans to make sure the hand-out man hasn't tossed out his stack, or, and this is better, the boss sends a lackey to pretend to be an ordinary pedestrian. If the hand-out man is there and makes an aggressive groin attack, the boss can feel good about the hire.

Sometimes I liked to talk to the hand-out man. "Good chicken?" "Yes, good." "What do you get with it?" "Fries." "A drink?" But other times you just shut up, because the hand-out man is anxious to get back to work, and you can't fault a guy for that. Only an asshole is going to give the hand-out man a hard time.

I was supposed to work at the liquor store in the afternoon, selling to boozers, recommending red wine to white people. But the city looked so great, and I wasn't sweating. My father's store was ugly, between his slapping me and his non-stop dusting of the stacked bottles, the alkies who mooched the one-ounce nips, and the rich people who shook their heads after I'd suggested the wrong wine for their five-course dinner party. I made the call.

"Hello?"

"Mom."

"Yes?"

"Mom, it's Josh."

"Hello Sweetie."

"I can't go to work today, Mom. Can you call him and

tell him?"

"Maybe you should call him, Honey." Gulp. Gulp. The sound of a vodkafall.

"I got to run, Mom."

"I think you should call your father, Joshua. He'll be upset."

"I got to go, Mom. Please call him. Bye."

"Sweetie. I don't know."

"May this Cathedral be worthy of God, worthy of the Catholic religion, and an honor to this great city." That's Archbishop John Hughes in 1858, at the cornerstone laying of St. Patrick's.

I was a member of a family that cared as much about its Jewishness as it did about the lint that gathers in washing machine filters and belly buttons. My father hated lint. The mezuza on our doorway had come with the apartment, and we passed it thousands of times without thinking about it. My father probably associated Jewishness with education (Genius Uncle Saul), achievement (Genius Uncle Saul), and his parents (Those Who Love Genius Uncle Saul). I got the same explanation for every Jewish holiday. Commemorates the flight of Jews from Egypt, my father would say, now shut up. I couldn't figure out why, if it was such a big deal being in Egypt, the Jews kept returning and leaving, returning and leaving, giving us all these different holidays commemorating each time they left.

My mother's grandfather had been a famous rabbi in Russia, but I had no idea what my mother thought about Jewishness, or anything.

I entered St. Patrick's through the bronze doors, leaving behind the motors and bodegas, and took the seat I'd claimed for my own when I first started coming, age 14. The back pew, past the statue of St. Peter, past the gift shop and holy water font. I often thought that the rows of candles, not three feet behind me, would ignite my head. A flaming Jew in St. Patrick's. Wouldn't help the Christian-Jew dialogue. But it never happened.

The pews were filled with the believers and the homeless, people like me, and obnoxious tourists with flashing cameras. A female cop strolled up and down the aisles to make sure the homeless didn't stretch out on the pew or start a fire to warm up a can of beans. I never put my feet on the knee-rests. I must have seemed like a true believer to the church cop, even though I never knelt and was careful not to put my hands together prayer-wise or mumble to myself. I sat quietly, respectfully. I didn't want to mock the serious people. And they were there, sprinkled throughout the pews, people who actually came to pray, mostly women who interlocked their fingers and put their heads on their hands and stayed that way for five or ten minutes before standing up, crossing themselves, and exiting through the bronze doors into the loud, violent world.

The choicest cut of St. Patrick's was in front and to the right of me, the candle rows. Men and women would put a few coins or a dollar in the box — the honor system does well in church — and pick up a short candle. With the candle in its metal case, men and women, using a short stick, would borrow fire from an already lit candle and illuminate their own, in memory of someone or something, on a special occasion, because they felt right doing it. They'd stare up at the holy figures and sometimes they'd nod like they were in a conversation, and they understood what the other guy was saying.

The old man's hand shook and the dollar bill was crunched up so small it could have fit in a thimble. It took him five minutes to unravel it. He could have given a quarter, which required no unraveling, or nothing at all, but he'd started giving a dollar 40 years ago, when his hand was steady, and he wasn't going to stop now. His left hand bracing his right, he lit the stick and tried to do the same with his candle, but the shaking was fierce. I thought of helping him. Finally, the glow topped his candle, and the wall of candles was a bit brighter. He blew out the stick. Didn't put his hands together or kneel. Just stood there, staring up. Nodded. He pulled a handkerchief from his pocket and patted his face. This was his quiet conversation with his God. He didn't need a mass or a Priest telling him what to do. He believed in something, and I didn't believe in anything.

I looked at the pulpit, the statue of St. Patrick, and the Liturgical Altar, where I imagined having sex with Gina, who'd been looking at me goofy-eyed the last week of school. I slept.

A naked Gina had been sitting on the archbishop's throne when I entered the church. We were alone.

"Come," she said.

I didn't take my eyes off her breasts as she jumped to the altar. Athletic. Bouncing. My clothes disappeared, and she giggled at the erection that seemed two pews ahead of me.

"Hi," I said, continuing my walk.

"Hey, Josh."

I knelt on the steps. Her belly was flat and coated with sugar. I looked up and saw her face, her smile that was warm with the glow of a thousand candles, all the candles in the church. She sat on the top step, her legs wrapped around me. She pulled me up and toward her. I entered her — the warmth of the candles — just as my father rose from the crypt behind Gina. He, too, was naked. Gross. "Jacob," he said, quietly. He wasn't looking at me, but behind me. I checked. No one. I turned back. My father was gone and Gina was back on the throne, buttoning up her blouse. She seemed satisfied.

The great organ, all 7380 pipes, shocked me and several others in the church out of sleep. Arms were stretched awake above the pews. I wondered who Jacob was, probably someone who led the Jews out of Egypt or brought them back or led them out the second, maybe third, time.

The organ player was practicing, playing a lick from one song and then abruptly changing keys, rhythm, and melody. Maybe he was just making sure each of the pipes was clear.

"I've been to the finest schools," the organist tells me. "Juilliard, Berklee. I've studied under genius."

"Are you Catholic?"

"Is there anything more glorious than the organ? Listen."

"Sounds good."

"Glorious."

"But are you Catholic?"

"I believe in the magic."

"The Catholic magic?"

"The magic in the music, and the music that's in me."

"Isn't that the Lovin' Spoonfuls."

"Love 'em."

I saw her again. The tall thin woman, dressed in black,

with dyed blond hair. She was walking up the center aisle, looking at the pews to her left and right. You couldn't help but notice her tiny mouth. And that she was upset. Our eyes met, and she continued past me. She walked to the information booth, said something to the seated woman, who shook her head. She thanked the seated woman and pushed the bronze doors to the outside.

This was a new experience for me, seeing a person after I'd thought I would never see 'em again. I walked over to the information booth.

"Excuse me." The woman was trying to memorize the names of the church's statues, which she'd written on a piece of loose-leaf paper.

"Yes, dear." She was a poster child for periodontal disease, but even in her broken smile you could see that she meant well.

"I'm not a Catholic, but I was wondering something."

"Yes?"

"Do you believe in coincidence."

"Coincidence?"

"You know, do you believe that everything is the work of God or are there things that just happen, you know, randomly."

"Well, I think that if everything were God's work we would not have all these confessionals here." I didn't get it, and it showed. She went on. "People act on their own, but they answer to God, do you see?"

"Yes, but what about things like weather or bumping into one person again and again on the street?"

"That's a good question, but I'm afraid I don't know. You might want to talk to one of the Sisters. I'm just a volunteer, you see."

"That's okay," I said. "One more question?"

"Sure."

"Do you know who Jacob was?"

"You mean, from the Bible?"

"Yeah."

"I believe he was Isaac's son."

"What was he like?"

"I don't really remember. I think one of the sons was good and the other was bad."

"But you don't remember which?"

"No."

"What about Isaac?"

"He was the son of Abraham, but I don't recall much more. I guess I should reread my Bible." She blushed and rattled off the list of statues. "I'm much better with the New Testament, you see."

"Who was that woman who just came up to you, do you mind my asking?"

"She was looking for a friend. Will you excuse me?" Polite but insistent.

Jews and jewelry. Jewry and Jewelry. From St. Patrick's, home of the Catholics, to 47th Street, the street of diamonds, workplace of the Jews. The merchants were sweating in their black suits. Curls clung to the wet cheeks of the boys. When a man took off his hat, if he wasn't bald, his hair was moist and flat. Everybody moved. Running to deliver a shipment, rushing to make a deal, to meet a customer or seller.

A couple of black guys, city workers with orange hats and cordless phones, had roped off a manhole. They disap-

peared into it for a few minutes, climbed out, and talked
about what they'd seen. They didn't seem to feel out of place,
even though the Jews looked at them suspiciously. No doubt
racial. But maybe it was more than racial, the way the Jews
lowered the glasses on their long noses to peer at the black
men. Maybe the Jews saw a ruse. Guys pretending to be
city workers, when they were really casing out the under-
belly of the diamond exchange for a heist. Moles. Digging
tunnels. Blacks going after Jews. Needed to rob. Couldn't
make an honest buck. No, it was definitely racial. So much
for the black-Jewish dialogue.

The shops in the exchange were packed like I'd never
seen them. Jews everywhere, a Jewish circus, men and
women standing at their stalls, speaking Yiddish, Hebrew,
and Russian to each other over the heads of customers who
roamed the aisles thinking one guy's deal could be beaten
by his neighbor. It was diamond day.

The best businessmen and -women in the city. They
would see a young man and they'd know. Engagement ring.
If he happened to glance at a diamond, without even stopping at the stall, just moving with the traffic, the stall operator, seemingly busy with a billion details and noises,
would ask if he needed some help. Got a good deal. What
are you looking for? Engagement ring? Look at these beau-
ties. So, when are you getting married. Hey, Mazel Tov, con-
gratulations. Where you going on your honeymoon? Fantastic. So, how many karats are you thinking? Big wedding?
And so on. It's not as though you bought something before
you knew it, but you did make a friend, and friends help
friends, right? If you walked away from your friend, said
you would catch up to him some other time, you felt like
shit. And when you glanced back as you turned the circus

corner — you had to glance back — the vendor would either be making friends with a new young man, which would make you feel wise, or he'd be staring at you, to see if you'd buy from another diamond man and spit on the friendship.

"Just browsing, thanks." I said this at every stall. Unless you want to make a thousand friends and lose them as fast, you have to say you're just browsing. So what if no one takes you seriously. At least you don't feel like shit.

The sun was still out, peeping from behind the skyscrapers like a kid who parts the curtains to check out the audience at his first school play, and you could see that folks leaving their jobs were thrilled by the brightness. They wore sunglasses. Some of them would walk home instead of taking the subway or bus. It's a shame, I thought, that so many people have to spend the day, the time when you can see things, inside. Of course, if you switched work to night, everyone would sleep during the day. So it's a wash.

I hadn't spoken to my father all day. He really didn't need me at work, but he liked to have me around, to slap and yell at. I bet he was cursing me, out loud. And I bet that, while he was cursing, he was scrubbing or dusting or mopping, the bastard. I was glad to be in New York City. Anywhere else, in a small town with one general store where everybody goes, a father can track down a son. Not in New York. God bless the Big Apple. I wasn't his son when I wasn't in his sight.

My favorite Chinese restaurant was Wok's, a great name. Imagine an American restaurant being called Pot's or Pan's. Never happen.

I'd go to Wok's once a week, thanks to the money of Genius Uncle Saul, usually after one of my midtown tours. It looked like every other Chinese restaurant. Same Chinese calendars on the wall, same fake paper shades over the hanging lights, same miniature bottles of soy sauce on the tables, same Chinese zodiac place mats telling me I was a smart pig.

I was a regular, a guy who liked a particular table and always ordered the chicken chow mein, heavy on the crispy noodles. And a Coke. It's a funny thing when you start being a regular somewhere. You want the folks there to know your name, and you want to know theirs. So you say, "By the way my name's Josh," which sounds a little strange, because it comes out of nowhere. At first, when I told Mrs. Chung my name, she didn't tell me hers. She nodded and smiled and took my money and said she looked forward to seeing me again.

For the first few weeks after I'd told her my name, Mrs. Chung had refused to use it, so, after paying my check one day, I said to her, "You know, my name's Josh. I'm wondering what your name is. Just so we can say hello to each other every week." Mrs. Chung looked as though I'd asked to inspect her genitals. But I kept smiling and looked so nice — I couldn't have worked for the Genitalia Inspection Office. "Chung," she said. "Mrs. Chung. Mr. Chung in kitchen in back." I always made a point of saying "Hello, Mrs. Chung" and "Goodbye, Mrs. Chung" and, after a couple of weeks, she started using my name. I'd become a regular.

There were a few people eating at Wok's, a couple of

businessmen who had decided to eat before going home and a family of tourists — Germans, I thought, judging by the blond hair, loud voices, and ugly throat sounds they made.

"Hello, Mrs. Chung."

"Hello, Josh. How are you?"

"Good, thanks. How 'bout you?"

"Fine, fine. A beautiful day, yes?"

"It's amazing. Have you been out at all?"

"No. But it very sunny. I see."

"That's a pretty blouse."

She beamed proudly. "Lord & Taylor. Forty dollar."

"It looks nice on you."

"Thank you. Why your hair messy?

"It's always messy, you know that."

"You need haircut, and shave, too." She rubbed her olive cheek.

"Yes. One of these days. I promise."

"Good." She had a way of talking that made everything sound like a deal had been struck. "You eating today?"

"Don't I always eat?"

"Yes." She laughed. "Your table all ready."

"Great."

David, Mrs. Chung's youngest, was on duty, and I said hello to him, using his name, as I walked to my window table. As always, I hoped that he wouldn't bring me a menu, that he knew I wanted chicken chow mein, heavy on the crispy noodles, and a Coke. He brought me a menu.

There she was again — outside, not three feet from me. She looked in the window and saw how empty the place was. The Germans, the businessmen, and me. She came in. Mrs. Chung led this tall, tiny-mouthed, worried-looking woman to the table next to me. Funky day.

She sat down slowly and ran her fingers through the short blond hair that had begun to show its dark roots. Her eyes were closed when David brought over a menu and glass of ice water. She took the glass and downed the water in just a few gulps. She had high cheekbones, a long nose, and strong, piano-playing fingers. No jewelry. No makeup. There were dark circles under her eyes. I thought she was in her early thirties, and should have been sleeping well, unless she had one of those sleeping disorders.

I ate my chow mein without looking at it. I was checking out my neighbor. David asked if everything was okay with my meal. I wanted to get my neighbor's attention, so I spoke.

"It's great, David. Thanks. Let me ask you something. How long does it take to cook chow mein?"

"Cook?"

"You know, make it."

"Five minute, maybe."

"Really? Wow, that's good."

"It good?"

"Yes, thanks." She hadn't looked up once.

David stopped next to her. I didn't think she'd opened the menu.

"Ready?"

David and I had a hard time hearing her. Her voice was low-pitched. Blended in with everything around it and easily got lost. David got the order by leaning over her. He brought her the food, all appetizers, which was a safe choice, a good choice. Chinese restaurants rarely screw up egg rolls, dumplings, and spareribs. She mouthed a "thank you." She put a sample of each food on her plate and poured an entire saucer of duck sauce over everything. She looked up and over her shoulder, for David, for more duck sauce. I had a full saucer on my table.

"Would you like my duck sauce?" I leaned over a chair. She looked at the saucer and then at me. She didn't recognize me from St. Patrick's.

"No thanks, I'll wait. Thanks though." My duck sauce was clean, but she didn't know that. In New York City you can't be sure that your neighbor hasn't drooled or spit into the sauce. Or worse. I would have done the same.

"You really like that stuff, huh?"

"Yeah."

Jesus. Did I sound like I was trying to pick her up? What an idiot.

She got David's attention, held up her empty saucer, and he brought her another helping. She poured half of it onto her plate.

I'd finished my chow mein and was sipping my Coke, trying not to stare at her, trying not to look like the type of freak who hangs out at a Chinese restaurant after finishing a meal. You don't have coffee at a Chinese restaurant, you shouldn't have dessert, you should just leave. That's the way it works.

"Excuse me. I don't want to sound like an idiot, but, I'm sorry, I don't want to interrupt your dinner."

"No, it's okay."

"Well, it's just been real weird. Three times today I've seen you, in completely different areas, the park, St. Patrick's, and now here. That's never happened to me before and, you know, in a city this big, you don't expect it to happen. I mean, if we were both tourists going to tourist traps, I could understand it, seeing you so many times, but, well,

I'm not a tourist, are you?"

"Nope. I live here."

"I mean, I saw you in the Park, by the ball fields, and I didn't think anything of it. And again, in St. Patrick's. You were walking up the center aisle. And now here, in Wok's."

"I've never been here before. Pretty good." She stuck half an egg roll in her mouth. She wanted the conversation to stop.

"I just wanted to tell you how weird I thought it was. I'm sorry, you go on eating." I signaled to David for the check. I wanted him to take his time, as much as I wanted the woman to speak.

"It is kind of weird." Yes! "Usually you're pretty safe writing off strangers." She thought like I did.

"It's a great part of the city, isn't it? I come around here all the time."

"My boyfriend and I do, too. He really loves it." She didn't smile, the way you expect people to when they talk about boyfriends or girlfriends. She didn't look at me. I hoped she didn't think I was a creep trying to pick her up. She could handle that, sure. Would call a bar creep a bar creep. But I didn't find her sexy. I was curious, that's all.

"Yeah? You guys live around here?"

"No, you?"

"Fifty-ninth and First."

"So you work around here?" She mopped her face. She wanted to go.

"Uptown a bit."

"What do you do?" It hit me. She thought I was an adult, an employed adult. No way did she see me as 16. Thank God I hadn't shaved, and that I had some size.

"I work in a liquor store."

"Oh." My job didn't impress her, and it shouldn't have. She waved David over and asked for her check.

"I mean, I'm an actor, but I work in the store to make ends meet." The lie didn't do anything. She put her fifteen bucks on the table and stood up.

"I got to run. See you around." And she walked out, with those interesting words.

"Delicious, Mrs. Chung." She was checking an invoice that she'd pulled from underneath the cash-register drawer.

"You like, Josh?"

"I always like your food." She took my money. "Can I use your phone?" She patted the receiver twice. Yes.

"Mom."

"Hello, Sweetie."

"Mom, I'm going to sleep over at Billy's tonight."

"Hold on, Honey. Daddy wants to say something to you."

"Where the hell were you today?"

"I didn't think you needed me. I called Mom."

"I'll make the decision if you're needed, Jesus Christ. Goddamned Raoul dropped a whole fucking case of Zinfandel in the basement."

"I'm sleeping over at Billy's tonight. I'll call tomorrow."

"You be at work tomorrow. You better be there, Joshua." It was always weird when he used my name. I mean, do boxers use each other's names in the ring? "Take this Mohammed." "Take that Joe."

I didn't pay much attention to Billy that night, which was okay, because he didn't pay much attention to the world, including me, that night. His family lived a couple of blocks from mine, and we'd gone to school together until the ninth grade, when a private school on the west side rewarded his brain with a scholarship. Everyone near Billy knew he deserved it, math-wise. He seemed to have every number in his head, spinning like clothes in a dryer, and he'd throw the right one out, the right answer, almost as soon as the math teacher got done asking the question. Math was the only subject he did really well at, but that was enough. The English and history teachers had understood early on that Billy was a math guy and that he would go far and that they shouldn't go overboard if he was less than brilliant remembering rules of grammar or why 18th-century Americans had given England the finger.

Billy didn't look like a numbers whiz. With full, wavy blond hair, blue eyes and a sweet, wide smile, he surprised folks who didn't know him. They saw a sports hero or heartthrob or future news anchor. Thing is, Billy stopped growing when he was 14, and at that age he was no more than five-two. So, to strangers, he became the sports hero who'd never be big enough to play ball, the heartthrob who, standing, would never be tall enough to kiss a full-grown woman on the lips, the news anchor who'd need to sit on a phone book or two in order for the television camera to pick him up.

He started smoking pot when he was in eighth grade, and he took to it. It was a good thing that he transferred to the private school, because at my school he would have gotten into the big-league drugs that would have crunched his brain. And he had a great brain. He wasn't as smart when he was stoned, but he could still do math. Hell, he'll be doing math in his coffin.

Billy's mom buzzed me up and met me at the door. She worked two jobs to support Billy and his younger brother. The older brother, Jay, had been out of the house a few years. She shopped in my father's stores because Billy and I were such good friends, and it hadn't taken her long to see the kind of guy my father was and to understand why I often slept over at her apartment. I never needed to call. I could just show up.

Billy was in his room, lying on his bed, stoned, reeking of pot, listening to Zeppelin's first, drawing on a big, white piece of cardboard.

"Yo."

"Hey Josh."

"What's up?"

"Not much."

"What you doing?"

"Drawing."

"Let's see." It was a picture of the number eight, falling onto its side.

"Why on its side?"

"That's the sign for infinity."

"Cool."

"Your father acting up again?"

"I've been walking around all day. I just didn't want to deal with him."

Billy smoked a joint. His mother didn't mind. She sometimes did it, too, to unwind after her evening stint at the video store. Besides, Billy continued to do well at school. He wasn't called a prodigy anymore, like he had been in the public school, but he was still the top dog in math.

I rarely smoked with Billy. Pot just slowed life down for me and, if anything, I wanted it to speed up. They ate rice and beans for dinner. I told them about the woman I'd seen all over the place. Billy didn't care that much. I was surprised. Thought he'd say how improbable it was, and give me the numbers to show it. At least his mom bit.

"So, did you make any sense of it in the end?"

"Not really. She left the restaurant real fast, before I got to know why she was where she was."

"I once picked up a hitchhiker, I think it was right outside Detroit, and dropped him off in Dayton, where I was staying for the night. The next day, coming back to New York, I saw the same guy standing on the highway in western Pennsylvania."

"Did you stop?"

"You know, at first I didn't. I thought it was kind of weird. Then I felt bad. I had picked this guy up before and he was nice enough. So about a quarter mile past him I stopped. And I remember waiting there for him, because I was too scared to back up on the shoulder, and he was taking a hell of a long time catching up to me."

"Did he?"

"Oh yeah. He got there eventually and we had a big laugh over it."

After she went to work, Billy and I watched TV, a thousand shows. Billy held the remote, and I think he just liked to see the digital numbers change on the cable box. We didn't talk much. Occasionally he'd ask if I was hungry. I was thinking about the woman, the duck sauce, the fact that she and her boyfriend hung around the same places I did. And how she hadn't smiled when she mentioned him.

I counted my money. Thought about poor, paroled Raoul dropping a case of Zinfandel. My father wouldn't touch him because Raoul had a bad habit of hurting people who touched him. I counted again. It wasn't that I'd decided to run away. I'd just decided not to return.

The sun was out again, and though I wore the same underwear, socks, and jeans, I borrowed one of Billy's T-shirts and felt nearly as comfortable as the day before, maybe eighty percent. I didn't visit Jane. I wanted to see the duck-sauce lady again. I wasn't obsessed or anything. She just gave me a goal at a time when I didn't have any.

Young men with mustaches, always mustaches, stood behind their carts, hawking both hot and iced coffee, muffins, and bagels. In the wings, along the park's access roads and paths, the hot dog men, always older and with accents, unhinged their carts from the cars and vans that had trailored them. The large umbrellas, once fitted into their metal holders, were opened. The propane heaters were fired up. The dogs boiled. The pretzels soft and warm. Soda on ice. Ready for business.

She wasn't there, so I headed south, past the Plaza and all the limos. The drivers, gathered around one car, smoked cigarettes and shared a laugh about a tabloid story, as they waited for their foreign clients and the leather luggage. Horses, hooked to carriages, accepted the gentle pats of passing children, as the Irish drivers tried to sucker tourists into a twenty-minute tour of the Park, costing only a billion dollars, but including a romantic description of Cork County and a spiel about how horses enjoy lugging 1500 pounds on scorching city days and how car exhaust isn't that bad for them.

There are a lot of bums in St. Patrick's in the morning,

when the shelters let out, when folks on their way to work can't help but stumble on the cardboard beds and wake the occupants up. The same woman was sitting at the information desk. I didn't think she remembered me. I sat in my pew, not intending to fall asleep or stay long. Several women in business suits and sneakers had stopped in on their way to work for a quick candle-lighting. The place seemed darker than usual. The sun wasn't high enough. The organ player wasn't there. Neither was the duck-sauce lady.

Wok's was closed. I had no idea what Mrs. Chung did in the morning.

I always walked up the middle of the New York Public Library's 28 outside steps, between the lions and the urns. I'd go to the library whenever I could, not because I was a big book fan, which is what Jane was hoping for, but because the book delivery system is one of the best things going in New York. You enter the building, and take the stairs to the third floor, occasionally looking down on the main, marbled hall. You're disappointed by the McGraw Rotunda on the third floor because, although it's nice to come upon a room of wood after seeing so much cold stone, the murals on the walls and ceiling, the work of Edward Laning, look like big comic book illustrations. Cheap. But you shake that disappointment off, if you know what comes next, the catalogue room, where the book delivery process is begun.

I picked one of the hundreds of title books lining the room and, letting the book open itself on a table, I looked up at the ceiling and lay the point of my finger down somewhere in the center of the page. It was a French title, something with "coeur" in it. It didn't matter of course. I wouldn't have read anything, even something I could understand. After filling out the order paper, I handed it to a young black woman, who sent it on its way, into a brass pneumatic tube, into the bowels of the earth, home of eight floors of stacks, 88 miles of books, and dozens of human gophers. Other libraries, of course, make you do the stack search, and I suppose that has its fun. But in New York, the best part is imagining what happens with your book order under the city. I always wanted to see a cross-section of the library, like they do with aardvark homes on nature shows. The gopher gets the order, finds the book, places it on the dumbwaiter, which rises to me.

I took the numbered ticket that the black woman had given to me into the Reading Room, where I joined other eager book-wanters sitting on a wooden bench in front of the number board. When your number flashes, you're on. 24. 18. 26. Sometimes the numbers don't run in order. 28. 30. 34. I held 32. The numbers ran up to 42 before mine was lit up. I thanked the man for my volume of French poetry and took a seat at the end of a table, next to a woman who was actually reading, and had at least ten books beside her left elbow. I looked at the words in my book, closed it, and watched the young and old in the Reading Room read.

The duck-sauce lady entered the room and sat, ticket in hand, in the exact place on the wooden bench where I'd been. It happened like that.

She got her book, a big one, and walked down the aisle toward me. I pretended to read. That was a first.

"Hey." I looked up. She had spoken to me. "Pretty amazing, huh?"

"Tell me about it."

"Anyone sitting there?" She pointed at the seat across from mine.

"No, go ahead."

Her book was about guitar-making.

"You build guitars?"

"I'm trying. I don't know yet if I'm any good at it. What do you got?"

"Some French poetry."

"Ah, *vous parlez français.*"

"Huh?"

"You speak French?"

"No." Then I lied. "They brought me the wrong one."

The woman next to me peered over her stack of books and crunched her face like a piece of plastic tossed in a fire. "Shhh." The duck-sauce lady and I retreated into our books. But mine was French poetry, and, of course, I knew nothing about either. I stroked my rough, two-day beard.

"I'm gonna have a cigarette. You want to get some air?"

"Sure."

We both got up. We were the same height. I walked ahead of her, turning every few steps to make sure she was following. I dropped my book at the delivery desk. She had left hers on the table. Once in the catalogue room, we were side by side. Once on the stairs, we spoke again of how weird it was, in a city this big, to continually run into each other. Once in the heat outside, we sat on the steps. And once my cigarette was lit, we introduced ourselves. Joshua Lipkin meet Tiffany Elizabeth Mann. Manny. Hello. Hello.

2

I would learn a lot about this woman, that she lived on the upper west side, never understood the bidding conventions of bridge, wrote ads for a living, built things out of wood, that she had few friends, not because she smelled but because you only a need a few people in this world and you hope that the few you have are good. She was vulgar. Her father was dead. There was a dog who peed on the floor. She wanted to have control over her life, but control was something she hadn't had in a while, like cod liver oil. She'd nicknamed herself Manny.

I would learn that her boyfriend had disappeared.

Before all of that I learned about how she cried. We sat on the library steps, her purse between us, which I took as a sign of trust. She asked me why I wasn't at work.

"I'm off today." I wondered if I'd have to call my father every day to tell him that I wasn't going to show up. Or whether I could call him once and say I wasn't going to show up again. Period.

"What about you?" She coughed loudly and violently, as if there was a chunk of sirloin stuck in her throat. But there wasn't, no steak. This was the way she started to cry, and the tears didn't drip from her eyes, but jumped, and it took only a few seconds for them to fan out and wet her cheeks. Some collected in the corners of her tiny mouth. Others took a wider route to her chin, before leaping onto the step between her legs. I think she was trying not to make any noise. She kept her mouth closed. But she needed to breathe, and she did it through her nose, pushing phlegm out both nostrils. She wiped her face with the back of her hand, which didn't absorb any of it. She was wearing a tee-shirt.

"Hang on." I ran down the steps to the hot dog man and asked for a couple of napkins. He scowled at me, like I'd returned a dog, saying it tasted like shit. Just a couple of napkins, come on. Finally, he motioned to the canister, and I took a lot more than two. I didn't even thank the bozo.

I wasn't used to crying. My mother didn't cry. She watched television. My father cleaned. Ours was a dry household, but only in the crying sense of the word.

"Thanks." She talked into the paper. "God damn it. Fuck." I was a fan of vulgarity, particularly in women, who probably have a harder time talking tough in a world that keeps telling them they need to talk nice. My English teachers always said cursing was a cheap way out of saying something with meaning, saying something properly. But "fuck" by any other name ain't the same. There's no proper way to say it, right?

"Is it your job?"

"No. I mean my job sucks, but that's not it. Jesus, I hate to cry." She blew a wad of phlegm into a napkin. Sounded like it could have been that chunk of sirloin after all. "It's something else, another part of my fucked up life."

A tall African man wearing jeans and a billowy purple turtle-neck hanging down to his knees squatted on the step in front of us and unloaded junk from his pockets and off his shoulders. Watches. Ribbons. Purses. Beads. He looked at her, noticed she'd been crying, and turned to me, thinking that a trinket would cheer up this sad, sad lady. I said no, and he said he had a good deal. He took one of his watches and thrust it at my face, like the hand-out men do with their pieces of paper. But not as effective. I leaned back. No thanks. I never saw these guys sell anything. Sometimes a tourist family would stop, and the mother would hold up one of the purses, but the father would remind her of the warnings he'd read about in the guide book, how most of the stuff is just crap. How did these guys live? Probably didn't need to eat much, but even rice and beans cost something. And where were the women? You never saw the women. Or kids.

"So what's wrong? You wanna talk about it?" This didn't sound like me, but there was nothing else to say. She put her elbows on the step behind us, arched her back, and I could make out the clumsy material of her bra.

"You have a cigarette?" I gave her one and lit it. The moisture on her face glowed. "It's my boyfriend."

I knew it, from the dinner at Wok's. So what could it be? Affair? Pregnancy, or his being an asshole about it? Dumping her? Pressuring her to do something or not to do something? Telling her he hasn't gotten over his other girlfriend, who's just moved back to the city from Paris and has announced that the love is still there?

"What's up?"

"He's disappeared."

"What do you mean?"

41

"I can't find him. He's just completely vanished."

"What? He hasn't called you or something? He's not answering his phone?"

"No. No." I'd been looking at her and she'd been looking at the step, maybe at the spots of tears. Now, she turned to me, and I could see it was something more serious. Her eyes widened, and became wet, and swelled, and I got set for another cry. But it didn't come. She talked.

She and Patrick had been in midtown, doing the same thing they did every week, the same thing they loved to do. It was like me and my tours, only they hit different spots. They'd walked from the upper west side, through the park, after both of them had finished work.

It had been warm, but not so bad that they didn't want to hold hands. They passed the Plaza, knowing they would soon return for a drink in the Oak Bar, where you tolerate the five-buck-a-bottle beer because it's pretty in there and everybody likes to treat themselves to a little something special every now and then, even a beer that costs two bucks more than down the street. Dinner was at a little Italian place on 51st, where they did a mean striped bass and risotto.

I asked her about risotto.

It's rice, she said, only different.

They were regulars here, went every Friday, knew the maître d' by name, always got the same table (if it was available), the one in the middle of the room, not the corner, because they liked the activity around them, liked to be able to look in all directions.

Had a great meal. Talked about a friend of Patrick's whose wife had cancer. It didn't look good. Young folks who'd wanted a family. Manny said she felt lucky, having Patrick. He squeezed her hand. The restaurant was unusually noisy, but it hadn't bothered them. They'd gotten their table and the people who were making most of the noise were a bunch of models — tall gorgeous women who were used to people looking at them. Patrick didn't drool, just made a funny comment about one of them having spaghetti sauce on her cheek and how none of her friends would say anything to embarrass her. Manny and Patrick left the restaurant just as the lightning storm hit.

No one had expected it. The weathermen had said clear and dry, and the people who believe in weathermen hadn't bothered to check their closets to make sure the umbrellas were where they should be. But the thunder cracked and you could actually see the lightning bolts weave between the buildings.

"A guy got hit in New Jersey. A golfer."

"Yeah?"

"Died. Right there. It was on the news."

I'd been at home, hadn't watched the news or even heard the storm, despite the open windows. I bet my mother had watched the news. Not that she understood any of it. My father liked rain because it cleaned the streets. But it also made dirt and paper and cigarette butts stick to your shoes, which sucked.

The rain had come down, only for about five minutes, but a lot of it. People leaving the restaurant and passers-by gathered under the restaurant's awning. You could barely see the people on the other side of the street. The rain gave everybody something to talk about, made it so folks didn't mind rubbing up against strangers. Most were laughing, not because the rain was funny, but because they all some-how realized how silly they must look, hiding from the water. And they didn't feel threatened by each other, as they would on a sunny day. Finally the rain let up and the streets steamed and the awning crowd dispersed.

Patrick and Manny were among them. He was through with the laughter, but the giddiness wouldn't let go of her, so even as he changed gear and said something serious about his work, how someone had cut his or her finger on an Exacto blade, she giggled, giggled as she watched the steamy streets and thought about how some people actually listen to weathermen.

"You know how you get that way sometimes?"

"Oh yeah." I didn't, of course. I'd never had a giggling problem.

Next stop, as always, was FAO Schwarz. Genius Uncle Saul used to take the cousins there in happier family days, when my father was closer to being a human, and my mother didn't drink vodka for breakfast. Two floors of fuzzy bears, flashing buttons, the biggest balls, widest hula-hoops, bleeps, buzzes, and boomerangs. Not to mention the guy standing outside, dressed like one of those marching wooden sol-diers, greeting everybody and trying to hide his embarrass-ment that he's decked out like a toy. Even adults love the store because they can leave, not feeling guilty that they haven't bought a goddamned thing. I often wondered if anybody ever bought anything there, like from the African guy. Maybe he and Mr. Schwarz nightly shared a can of beans, sitting at the entrance of the Lincoln Tunnel, talking about what they hadn't sold, hardened to the car noise and exhaust and the condescending stares of drivers and passengers.

Patrick and Manny said hello to the wooden soldier, who probably wanted to tell them that he was a regular Joe and needed to dress up to scrape out a living, to feed a kid or pay for school. They walked around the first floor, careful not to step on the children lying on the ground, wrestling with the stuffed bears, elephants, and kangaroos. They played a video game. Rode the escalator to the second floor, where Manny took control of a motorized steam shovel and used it to scoop up a fallen bunny that had run out of juice and had stopped jumping and wiggling its nose. As she did this, Patrick, about ten feet away, inspected the new art gadgets and toys. Patrick was a painter.

They crossed Fifth Avenue to Grand Army Plaza where, in front of the fountain of the naked lady, they always danced, had been dancing since the first time they came here, ten months before, when he had grabbed her, to her delight, did a little Fred Astaire back and forth, and let her spin solo, arms outstretched, staring at the sky and the whirling tops of buildings. Sometimes she spun until she got dizzy and other times until she felt that New York City was staring at her, and no one should be expected to deal with that. Patrick had started spinning too, several months ago, when she had boasted she could do better on the dizzy test. And she could.

That night there were only a few people around, a bum and a couple of old ladies who might have been reminiscing about the good old days, when pharmacies were small and candy bars cost a nickel. Manny didn't feel the city's eyes on her, so she would spin until she could spin no more. Patrick grabbed her unusually hard, but not enough to be scary, and they did the Fred Astaire back and forth, he leading, and then he let her go. She extended her arms, looked like the hand-out man, and rotated, slowly so as to last longer. She closed her eyes.

"Have you ever seen a girl spin?" an old lady asks me.

"No, but I've heard it happens."

"The world's their oyster."

"You sound like you don't like it."

"Like it? I'd like it if I was a Rockefeller and could afford to spin all day."

"You gotta be rich to spin?"

"Who else has the time? Most people need to work."

"You ever spin?"

"Never."

"Never?"

"Well, once. But that was at my cousin's wedding, after a glass of wine."

The noise, New York's own, came into sharper focus. Horses clip-clopped next to honking taxis. Manny opened her eyes and saw the peaks of the City — the skyscrapers, some of them lined with gold, the GM building, the empty space over the Park, the Plaza.

Could have been two minutes, could have been four, could have only been 55 seconds, Manny didn't know, but she had a feeling that a Grand Army Plaza record was being set. She gave up when her head started to bob and her legs started to give way, when the orbit went wacky, and she saw the tops of buildings one moment and the bottom the next and all sky the next. She stopped spinning and staggered, waiting for her brain to recover from the dirty trick she'd played on it. She turned to where Patrick had been spinning. He wasn't there.

"Wasn't there?"

"No."

She didn't think anything of it at first. Thought he was just temporarily out of her sight, in a shadow, behind the fountain, behind her, so she sat down on a bench. The old women were looking at her, but old people will look at young people. She gave it a couple of minutes, then she stood up and walked, calmly at first, around the fountain. No. She looked over by the horses. No. The limos. No. Back at FAO Schwarz. Southward. Again, around the fountain. No. Again, around everything. She looped around Grand Army Plaza, quietly calling out Patrick's name — she wasn't panicked. People will disappear for a few minutes in New York. You just hope the two of you aren't so separated that you need to head back to the apartment and wait for the call and the explanation and the relief and the laughter, and the disappointment that so much time had been wasted and the night's plans had washed out. She called out to the benches, to the fountain, to the limos. She walked behind the old women and then in front of them. She asked if they'd seen the man she'd just been with. "Tall, up to here. Blond hair down to there." They didn't answer. They moved closer together, frightened. "You know, the man who was just here, dancing with me, dancing like this." The old women had seen her spin. Crazy girl. Silence.

The bum was asleep.

"I began to freak."

"No kidding."

"I called his name louder and walked around faster and the City just seemed so empty. I ran across Fifth Avenue and up the stairs to FAO Schwarz. I asked the toy soldier if he'd seen Patrick. I said, 'the guy I came in here with 20, 25 minutes ago.' He looked at me like he'd never seen me. The whole city had gone dead. So I walked in. He wasn't on the first floor, by the video games, and he wasn't on the second floor, by the art gadgets. He was nowhere."

She must have fit in, seemed like a mother who'd lost her child to a stuffed animal in this corner or a talking computer in that. Probably happens a lot there. But she was looking for a grown-up, not a kid.

Grand Army Plaza had changed when she got back. The bum had awakened and wandered off, and the two old women, the stone-faced ones who'd stared but hadn't seen a thing, had left, too. A couple with a little girl was looking at the fountain — tourists, only tourists look at fountains at night. She walked up to them, and when they saw her right next to them, they recoiled, thinking she was out for money. She asked if they'd seen a young man, "tall up to here, blond hair down to there." Relieved that she hadn't plunged a knife into their hearts, but still concerned that there might be a con somewhere, the mother and father tucked their daughter securely between them. No, sorry. The girl said nothing, stared at Manny like the old women had done.

The Plaza was busy, but without Patrick. Same for the Oak Bar, where, if things had gone right, they would have been sitting, drinking, maybe kissing once in a while. She called Patrick's. His machine picked up after four rings, one of those long, rambling recordings, the voice telling you the obvious, that the person's not home but leave a message and you'll get a call. She left a message, more pissed off than frightened. "Where the hell are you?"

"You call the police?"

"Yeah. After I got home and waited for a while. They were a bunch of assholes. When I told them it was my boyfriend who was missing and that he'd only been missing for, what, three hours or something, they laughed."

"So what are they gonna do?"

"I called again yesterday, after he'd been gone all night and all morning and they said I could make some kind of formal missing persons report. But they don't give a shit. They think Patrick's on a drinking binge and is gonna show up vomiting on my stoop one of these days."

"What a bunch of idiots."

"I'm gonna go to the precinct now. It's been two days."

"Can I come?" Okay, so I sounded too much like an eager kid.

"You want to go to the police station?"

"It's better than sitting in the library and trying to read a book in a language I don't understand." True.

"Sure. If you want."

We got up and she said she was going to run back inside and return the book that she'd left on the table. I told her that they take care of stuff like that. She believed me, but said she liked to put away her things. Reminded me of my father and cleaning and order. Shit. I had to call my father. I told her I was going to make a call and would meet her back on the steps.

"Raoul."

"Hey, man, where the hell are you? Your dad's bullshit."

"Do me a favor, tell him I can't make it today and that I'm sleeping over at Billy's, will ya?"

"Whoa, Josh. I ain't tellin' papa Lipkin his boy ain't coming to work. I'll get him. Hold on."

"Raoul. Raoul."

"Joshua? You were supposed to be here half an hour ago. Do you know what I do to make this place run? Do you know how much food costs, how long I have to fuckin' work to pay for the fuckin' food you eat, do you?"

I pivoted the phone so that the mouthpiece was still in place, but the ear-part was hanging below my chin. I could just hear him screaming my name, and it made the distance between us more real, more comforting.

"I'm not coming to work for a few days. I'm going to be staying at Billy's." As I turned the phone right-side up, the screaming got louder, but Daddy was far enough away, and it was easy to hang up.

So, this Patrick guy had disappeared. You hear about missing people all the time, mostly kids who are stolen by divorced fathers or are kidnapped by strangers offering candy. These are the milk-carton kids. End up in the river or hacked up in a dirty apartment or buried in a shallow grave in Tennessee. But vanishing adults are a different breed. The stockbrokers who steal the retirements of little old ladies and buy a bungalow in the tropics and drink mango juice out of coconuts. Or the johns who fantasize about strangling a prostitute and one day, what the hell, decide to live out their fantasy. Or the two-bit hustler, a cocky son of a bitch, who thinks he can muscle in on the territory of a mob dude, without paying the price. No such luck.

But these are crimes, and the way Manny described it, Patrick wasn't the type to commit one or have one committed on him. I mean a big crime, a murder. Besides, the guy disappeared while Manny was doing her record-breaking 360s in Grand Army Plaza. Even if he'd been involved in something dark and messy, who would have had time, while

Manny was rotating, to jump Patrick and steal him away? If someone had smacked him on the head and dragged him away while Manny was spinning, someone would have heard something, someone.

He'd probably gotten nervous. Saw Manny spinning, freaked out about the relationship, maybe got jealous that she was lasting so long. Didn't have the guts to tell her. He bolted, leaving her frantic and dizzy. An asshole. That was the thing. She was spending all this time and energy looking for him, and when he turned up, he'd confess that he'd freaked out, and she'd see that he'd acted like a schmuck, and the whole shindig would be over.

I agreed with the cops. Patrick was drinking or hiding, maybe both. Gave men a bad name. He'd skipped out on Manny while Manny was spinning for joy.

I could have distrusted cops, even hated them. I'd never had any trouble, but I'd heard the stories. From Raoul, who admitted being a criminal, but said the cops always roughed him up more than they needed to. From Jamal, whom the boys in blue liked to hassle while ignoring the real crimes, the murders and muggings. Even from my father, David Lipkin. The cops would cite him when he used to block the sidewalk with barrels of mixed buttons. He liked to say that the Constitution protected his commerce. The cops would tell him, not as long as he was blocking the sidewalk. He said they were anti-Semitic. Now, my father's opinions never meant much to me, but they completed the circle, rounded out what I'd heard from people who weren't as idiotic.

Still, these negative feelings never took hold. I liked the guys with guns and shiny, black shoes. If one of them stood on the corner, waiting to cross the street, I'd weave through the crowd to stand next to him, hoping he'd greet me, that we could do some small talk. Same when one of them was sitting at the counter of the coffee shop on the corner. I'd sit next to him. Part of the appeal might have been that they didn't seem suspicious of me. I hadn't done anything wrong and, around me, they could feel comfortable taking their hats off and undoing the top buttons on their bullet-proof vests. Sure, some of them got carried away. Beat up folks. Stole from the till. Stole from the drug dealers to deal a little themselves. But they also got killed. And they drank a lot, because when you're looking over your shoulder all day, worried that someone might try to pop you, and when you're constantly touching your chest to remind yourself that the bullet-proof vest is there and wondering why it doesn't cover your head also, you need a good, stiff drink.

Manny and I walked into the 8th-Avenue precinct and I felt good that I hadn't done anything wrong. A lot of body contact, yelling, and running around. Most of the good guys were in uniform — the rest were the undercover, suited boys. There was typing, talking on the phone, grouping the bad guys, young men wearing T-shirts or muscle shirts. Some of them screamed that they were innocent, while others quietly sat on the benches, waiting for their lives to take another bum turn. Manny told the desk officer that she wanted to report a missing person, and the fat, red-faced alcoholic didn't even look up from the pile of papers he was stamping.

"Well?"

The guy turned his head around back.

"Hey, Rizzi, you gonna jerk off all day or you gonna help us out?"

Detective Rizzi either had a shrinking disorder or was a complete moron when it came to buying clothes, because his jacket was so big that he had to fold the sleeves into cuffs and the pants so big that, beneath the belt, they bagged up into clumsy folds and blew out over his thighs, looking like the pants worn by clowns and belly dancers. The clothes made his head look small, but I thought that without them it would have looked that way, too. He was nearly entirely bald, except for a few wisps in the center-top, like the hair sprouting from an onion. He had a small mustache and, on his left cheek, a football-shaped scar. Rizzi looked dumb, a guy who'd seen a lot and not understood any of it.

"Can I help you?"

"I want to report a missing person."

"Come on in."

He opened the swinging wooden door and led us to his desk in the corner. He even walked like a clown, with exaggerated, long steps. We sat down and he took out from his top left drawer a form, which he put in the black, manual typewriter. Cops know how to type.

"Okay, name?"

"Mine?"

"Yeah."

"Tiffany Elizabeth Mann, M-a-n-n."

"And who's this?" When he tilted his head toward me, I lost all confidence in my innocence.

"Me?"

"Oh boy, this is going to be a long day. Yeah, you."

"Joshua Lipkin. I'm just a friend."

"Just a friend." Rizzi made a note on a small white pad.

Manny gave her address and phone number.

"Okay, name of the person you claim is missing?"

"Patrick Henry."

"P-a-t-r-i-c-k H-e-n-r-y. Wait a second. That sounds familiar. Is he famous, an actor or something?"

Up to that point, I hadn't heard Patrick's full name. I remembered Mrs. Swanson teaching about Patrick Henry in freshman history. As soon as Manny gave Rizzi the name, I thought, just for a few seconds, that she'd made it up, made him up, fed me a wacky story because she was bonkers and did stuff like that. I mean, I didn't know her, we'd just plunged into this friendship, without the background of time spent together, without the opportunity for me to see if she really was bonkers. New York is full of loons. I would have felt really taken if she'd said Elvis Presley or John Lennon or something, but even Patrick Henry was enough.

"No, that's just his name. There was a guy in the Revolutionary War with the same name, but there's no relation."

"Revolution?"

"The American Revolution."

"Oh yeah, that's right. Wait, there's a guy here who knows everything about that. Hey, Bobby. Come here." Bobby was in uniform, young, about Manny's age.

"Yeah Rizzi?"

"Hey professor, I got a missing person here named Patrick Henry. That ring a bell?"

"You kidding me?" Bobby laughed.

"I ain't kidding you. Serious."

"'Give me liberty or give me death,' remember?"

"Oh yeah, that guy."

"They called him the Demosthenes of the Age."

"Demosthenes. What the hell's that?"

"A famous orator in Greece. So you got a guy named Patrick Henry, huh. I'll say he's missin'. Been missin' for nearly two hundred years."

"You mean dead."

"Yup." They both laughed.

"Wait a second, professor. Wasn't he also the guy who said, 'I got one life for my country' or 'give me a life and I'll give you a country,' or, wait, 'I regret there are lives in this country' or something like that?"

"No, idiot. That was Nathan Hale. He said, 'I regret that I have but one life to lose for my country.' He was an American spy."

"A spy?"

"A spy for us, against the British."

"Oh, that's all right." Rizzi jumped from his seat onto the desk (his jacket got caught under one of his shoes), put one hand on his hip, stretched the other into the air, and yelled, "I regret that my life is lost for my country. But give me liberty." He was ignored by some, booed by others, and applauded by an old woman sitting on the bench next to a row of quiet thugs.

"You idiot." Bobby walked away.

"Can we continue now? Jesus Christ."

"Easy does it, ma'am. Just tryin' to lighten the atmosphere a little. I didn't mean to upset you."

"All right, can we get this done with, please?"

"Yeah. So what's his relationship with you?"

"He's my boyfriend."

Rizzi threw me another suspicious look.

"And when's the last time you saw Mr. Patrick Henry?" He giggled when he said the name.

Manny told him the story as she had told it to me, minus some of the mood. Dinner. FAO Schwarz. Grand Army Plaza. Spinning. Disappearance. Search. Nothing. Search. Nothing. People at his job and in his building hadn't seen him since that day.

"How long you guys been together?"

"About ten months."

"Any problems?"

"What do you mean?"

"Well, you know, every relationship has its problems. I'm just wondering how things were going with you guys."

"Fine, I think. Listen, if you're suggesting that he needed to get away from me for some reason, he didn't have to do it like this. Jesus. We would have talked, figured something out."

"You know, sometimes men don't do a very good job talking, so they just get away, leave, for a few days. He comes back. You kiss. You smooch. Everything's okay."

"Listen, he's been gone for more than a day and a half. No one's heard from him. It's not what you think."

"People never think it is."

"Are you going to do something?"

"You've filed a report, and we'll follow procedure. You have any reason to be believe he's been involved in anything illegal?"

"Illegal?"

"Yeah."

"No."

"Nothing? No drugs or anything?"

"No, not at all."

"Okay. We'll be in touch. Oh, one more thing. How long have you two known each other?" Manny and I looked at each other.

"A day."

"A day?"

"Less than a day, really."

"Really?"

"Josh and I met at the library. I told him what happened, and he offered to come over here with me."

"I have your name, right?" Rizzi looked at his notes. "Lipkin. Okay, I'll give you a call, ma'am."

I looked back as we went through the wooden swinging door into civilian-land, and I saw Rizzi looking at me. Damn. You don't want to get caught looking at a cop who's looking at you. Messes you up.

"What a fuckin' freak show." Manny, it seemed, was pleased to leave the cop shop.

"Tell me about it. And I usually like cops."

She said she had some errands to do. I got the feeling she wanted some time alone, which didn't bother me.

"You want to meet later? You can tell me some more about Patrick. Maybe I can help somehow."

"Sure. I'll meet you at the Oak Bar at five."

"You sure you want to go there? I know you said you guys always went there, or go there." The problem of when to use the past tense had come up.

"Yeah. I like it there. The place actually makes me feel good."

"Okay."

"Bye."

I watched as she walked off uptown. Small steps for a tall woman. Looked like her legs were tied together at the knees. I headed east. I needed some clothes. David Lipkin, Daddy, would still be at work, so I could go home. That's how my head worked.

Part of my mother's problem was that her parents were much too old to have children. They tried for years, but grandma Hirshfield's body preferred miscarriages to babies, and every few months she faced another round of tears and grandpa Hirshfield's rantings that his wife was less than 100 percent woman. Finally, my mother grabbed grandma Hirshfield's womb and wouldn't let go, showing more aggressiveness than she ever would as an adult. There was a big party the night grandma came home from the hospital. Both parents fell asleep — she on the bed, he in a rocking chair — before dessert was served. Tired from age, not from all the birth activity.

They worked like dogs, cobblers whose store had once been a doughnut shop. They displayed the repaired shoes on racks that had previously held cinnamon-sugar sweets. And when they got home at night, when they climbed the stairs to their apartment, my mother would want to read and play games and wrestle with grandpa Hirshfield and braid grandma's hair and have grandma return the favor. But the folks only wanted to sip their soup and doze off. My mother's candle, the light that all kids have inside them, was snuffed out early in her life. They told her she would work, graduate from high school, make a man happy, and make as many babies as she could. She did work and graduated middle of her class.

The television was on and the volume was up full, some talk show about how certain folks like sex with animals, how even responsible, corporate executives go in for a little pig smooch once in a while. Her glass was empty, and a cigarette lay in the ashtray, having burnt down to the filter, which was beginning to smoke and send chemicals into the air. She was eating a piece of dry toast sprinkled with sugar, maybe thinking about the doughnut shop turned cobbler shop, about the kids who came before her and had eaten all the crullers they ever wanted.

"Hey ma."

"Josh, it's so hot, isn't it?"

"Why don't you turn on the fan behind you?"

"Okay." She leaned back without looking and repeatedly pressed the fan's off button. Frustrated, she forgot about the toast in her left hand and the sugar began to spill off onto the table and onto her lap.

"I got it, ma." The wind hit the back of her head, straightening curls and extending them in front of her face like a horse's blinders. Not that she needed them.

"That feels nice." She bit a piece of sugarless toast, and took in with it a few strands of hair, which she chewed, some of it breaking off into her mouth.

I put some clothes into my school bag and sensed that a period of my life was ending. I could have borrowed clothes from Billy. I could have bought some, courtesy of Genius Uncle Saul. But maybe I needed to come back one last time. I lay down on my bed, looking at the constellations, and I felt sad. I thought I had outgrown it, but I hadn't. I was falling asleep. It was a mistake, one that I couldn't help making.

It wasn't the fat man who woke me up, but the big man, David Lipkin.

"There's sugar all over the place."

My eyes opened to Orion and I jumped out of bed, grabbed my bag.

"Is your son here?" Quickly, I walked into the kitchen, toward the door. "What's your story? Where the hell have you been?" He grabbed my arm when I was next to him and squeezed so hard that I imagined the muscle breaking in two. Snap. I wouldn't look up into his face. "Answer me." I yanked my arm from his grip and with my other swung my bag at his face. Underwear, socks, and shirts don't weigh much, but the zipper caught his cheek. A zigzag line of blood. I ran out the door, tearing my shirt on the mezuza. I took the stairs in threes and fours.

When I hit the street, I caught my breath. "You son of a bitch. Joshua, get back here." My father was leaning out the window, a napkin on his cheek." I ran again. "Joshua. Joshua." He would spend the next hour painting himself with iodine. A shaving accident, he'd tell Raoul and customers. Not many customers would ask.

Manny had changed into a brown jumper. She was sitting at a table, sunken into one of the leather chairs, sipping a red drink, a bloody Mary, I guessed. It took a few minutes for my eyes to adjust. Your pupils can't open fast enough when you step from the day's brightness into the dark forest of the Oak Bar, where light, like the city's bums, isn't allowed. Sometimes rich folks like the sun, to tan under, and other times it's just common.

A short, black man came over and asked in accented English for my order. All the waiters were black, and the drinkers white — foreigners who'd stuffed their wallets with dollars and didn't care how much anything costs. In a place like this, you want to tell the waiter that you're a local, not just another tourist. You care more than they do. You want to share a laugh with the waiter. Boy, those Germans sure can drink, huh? How about them Japanese? Big on the scotch. But you don't do anything like that because the waiter is tired of having white guys, foreign or local, pretend that everybody's a buddy here, and that things like color don't matter.

On the western wall is a painting of the outside of the Plaza on a stormy night, with swirling wind and rain, and frustrated people who want to get to the ballet dry. And behind the bar is a painting of the fountain where Manny spun that night and where Patrick did his disappearing trick.

"You said you're an actor, right?" Gulp.

"Yeah. I mean, I try, but it's hard, you know, there are so many of them in the city."

"What have you been in?" I tried to remember the last play I'd read. *Romeo and Juliet*. Eighth grade. Mr. Frieder's class.

"*Romeo and Juliet*, but that was a while ago."

"Who were you?" I couldn't say Romeo. She'd ask too many questions, maybe ask me to recite some lines. I thought, there's a father in the play.

"Romeo's father."

"Neat. Where was it?"

"We did it at schools around the city, trying to get kids interested in theater." I was glad that I hadn't said off-Broadway, even way-off, because she might have known every little theater in the city, even the crusty ones in the Village. I drank half my beer. "Did you go home before?"

"Yeah."

"No sign of Patrick, huh?" She shook her head and finished her bloody Mary. A drop of red on her upper lip. It slipped into her mouth.

"You've been together ten months, you said?"

"Yeah, ten months. Around that."

"So, tell me about him."

There wasn't much to tell, she said. He was smart, talented, sweet. Things had been going great, which made Rizzi's point hard to believe. Patrick had come to New York from Massachusetts to go to art school, but he flunked out after two years because he stopped doing the work. One of those guys whose grasp exceeds his reach. He could paint beautifully, liked portraits while all the kids around him were scratching their canvasses with razor blades or gluing orange peels to them or painting a black rectangle inside a red one, that's all, and calling it a landscape. He didn't care, as the teachers wanted him to, about what was going on in the art world. He hated the art world. He'd see the stuff in the galleries and call it as he saw it. Shit. All the kids talked about who was showing where and what the inside jokes were in the paintings. Patrick didn't know any inside jokes, art-wise. The kids said his paintings lacked irony. He agreed and wondered what the problem was.

He worked his way up to manager at the hardware and lumber store. She'd always bought materials there — wood and tools — and he was very friendly, and cute, so she started going there even when she didn't need anything. She'd browse and he'd show her the new lathes and routers that had just come in. They'd appreciate precision tools and laugh at super-featured ones designed for people who don't know what they're doing but can't resist shiny, overpriced machinery. She'd buy wood by the sheet and he'd carry it for her. They'd talk about dowels and he loved her idea of establishing the country's first nail-gun target range.

"Who made the first move?"

"I did. I always do. The nice guys, it seems, are the quiet ones who won't say anything."

I was on my second beer. She, her third bloody Mary. We'd emptied two bowls of mixed nuts.

"You have a girlfriend?"

"No."

"Boyfriend?"

Whoa. I'm an actor (lie) so I'm gay.

"No, I'm straight. I just don't have a girlfriend now, that's all. You and Patrick hit it off right away?"

He loved her dog, the only boyfriend who, when he entered her apartment and saw Squeaky, fell to the ground and rubbed the animal's belly and went "cac, cac, cac" into her ear. Even when Squeaky peed on his shoe for the first time — she lost control when she got excited — he didn't get mad, just took the paper towel from an embarrassed Manny and cleaned himself up. Never stopped petting the dog, and the dog never stopped peeing, dripping really, and Patrick laughed and Manny joined him, paper towels in hand.

They cooked together, walked through Central Park, the Met, he took her to St. Patrick's.

"Why there?"

It's not that he was religious, but he could think there. Besides, it's beautiful. She thought he might have turned up there, and that's why she'd gone in the day before. Asked the woman at the information booth if she'd seen him.

He was generous, put up with her moods, which could go wild in all directions, let her be alone when she wanted. But she wanted to be alone less and less. He loved kids. Wanted a couple. That was better than six or seven, which would have meant that the woman was expected to do nothing else.

"Got a picture?"

She took out of her purse a small book on bridge — "You learning about bridge, Manny?" "Well, I don't know if you can call it learning." — and her wallet. Sticking out of one of the compartments was a lock of hair, blond. Manny pushed it back in and took out the photo. They were standing together. Same height. It was winter. She wore a parka and he had on a pea coat. He was blond — the same color as the lock in her wallet — and clean-shaven, and when he smiled he opened his mouth a little. I tried to find an answer in his eyes, a reason why he'd disappeared. Yes, I tried to see if there was a dark side that even Manny didn't know about. I couldn't find a thing. Their arms were around each other at the shoulder so they looked as much like pals as lovers. Manny finished her fourth drink, thudded her glass on the table, and waved our waiter over. Her mouth had begun to quiver and she was blinking a lot.

"Let's get out of here and go for a walk."

She tried to focus on me and looked skeptical. She started to cry, but not loudly or violently, as before. The water just built up. A light rain rather than a flood.

We paid our outrageous bill, which would have covered four chow meins at Wok's, and walked through the lobby and outside, where the strong wind pushed sweat back into your body and seemed to do the same with Manny's tears.

Children were playing around the fountain, splashing water and throwing pebbles at the statue of the naked woman, the lady carrying a basket of fruit. One kid plucked a dead pigeon from the water. His parents ran up and reprimanded him. They threw the bird back and cleaned off their son's hands. Think of the dirt on a New York City bird. Maybe the dirty pigeon had been taking a bath the night of Patrick's disappearance, when lightning cracked into the water and electrocuted the poor dear. Zap and sizzle.

I imagined that night, with Manny spinning. If she'd been going for a record-long time, as she said, maybe there would have been time for a band of thugs to jump Patrick, smack him over the head and drag him to their getaway car, parked next to the limos. But why wouldn't they have waited until he was alone in his apartment, why would they have risked being seen and caught? It would make sense if they were stupid. But if Patrick was into something bad, bad enough that a band of thugs would do this to him, you'd think the thugs would be professionals, and professionals wouldn't have gone after him then, while his girlfriend spun nearby, in the heart of New York City.

"I'm gonna go home."

"Where do you live?"

"Broadway and eighty-fifth."

"I'll walk with you. You want to walk? It's nice out."

"You know, we were going to go to Massachusetts in a couple of days. I was going to meet his parents."

"He'll turn up."

I looked up. Someone in one of the apartment buildings, who happened to be looking out the window, who happened to be looking with binoculars, would have seen the whole thing. The seagulls knew. The horses knew. Hell, the little old ladies who'd been sitting on the bench knew, but they were too afraid. I saw the wooden soldier standing at the entrance to FAO Schwarz. He probably knew. The dead pigeon had probably known, too, and was about to tell Manny, but was bumped off before it got the chance.

When I met Manny, I didn't know if I was a virgin.

Charlene was the first black girl I was attracted to and the first girl who let me touch her breast. She was light brown, a star athlete, a lightning-fast runner, and she walked as though, at any moment, she might break into a sprint. We'd seen each other around the neighborhood for years, and we met when I started playing basketball now and then with her brother, Jamal. She used to come and watch us play. Unlike Jamal, she wouldn't have anything to do with drugs, and when her brother started dealing, she told him that he'd become just another thug or a stat, a morgue number. But Jamal had nothing else. At least Charlene had the track, where she ran circles, or ovals, around anyone who challenged her. I'd go and watch her, and she amazed me, the way she controlled her body, pointed her hands and ran with long strides. The other girls, next to her, looked like babies who'd been hit on the back of the head and stumbled forward with arms flailing and eyes wide with fear.

We'd go to her apartment three times a week, when her mother was out working. The other days were down time, because I wouldn't bring her over to my apartment. She thought I was embarrassed, her being black and our being Jewish and Jews and blacks getting on about as well as milk and vinegar. But then people told her about my parents and she understood.

We were kissing one day when she took my right hand and placed it on her left breast. I must have shown some surprise — swallowed too loudly, mumbled something into her mouth, shaken — because she withdrew and smiled, said "it's okay," and kissed me again. I remember going under her shirt and not knowing how to take off her bra and feeling with my index finger under her bra and trying to take her bra off and her stopping me. She didn't want to go too far. Two of her friends were pregnant, and I think she believed there was a trip wire connecting her bra and panties. When one went, so went the other. But she let me slide my hand over the smooth bra and okayed my finger prying underneath every now and then.

She broke up with me because she felt the relationship was getting in the way of her sports. She needed to work harder for a scholarship and she needed a scholarship to get the hell out of there. She had more direction than any other kid I knew. We remained friends. I could understand her. I still went to the track and rooted for her. She always won. She'd get her scholarship.

The mystery of my virginity-loss went like this. Laurie was a year older than me and had probably had sex a thousand times with Sandy, the guy she'd been seeing since seventh grade but who, a few months before I entered the picture, had been put in jail because he liked to break into cars. She was as big as me, with long black hair that always looked dirty and a face that reminded me of the pictures of Pocahontas in our history books, even though she had no more Indian in her than I had in me. We were in her apartment, in the building next to mine, and General Hospital was on the tube. I think there had just been a fire or miscarriage or murder or kidnapping, when she laid back on the couch and pulled me on top of her. This was the first time I'd ever been horizontal with a girl, and I could feel my weight on her, maybe as much as she felt it. After kissing for a while and her letting my hands wander over her like a mouse snooping for cheese, she pushed me off her — the girl was strong — and went to the bathroom. She returned naked and told me that she had protection. Which was good. The one thing I was confident about. She knelt in front of the couch, undid my sneakers, pulled off my pants, my underwear, and again pulled me on top. With her hand, she was doing the work of getting me inside her. Problem was I ejaculated and I didn't know if I was inside her at the time. She said, "it's okay," and I couldn't figure if she meant that I was too fast or had fired in the wrong direction. She got up and again went to the bathroom. She came back with her clothes on, although they didn't seem to fit as well, like an apple skin glued back on the fruit. She was affectionate, despite what had happened, whatever had happened. I put my pants back on and she stroked my hair as we watched General Hospital.

Sandy got out of jail a week later and they got back together.

I'd never been in a one-bedroom apartment. My relatives lived in bunches and my friends lived in families, and all of us had at least two bedrooms. Not that there was enough space for any type of ball-playing, but you could go for a good walk and never open the door.

In Manny's apartment there was a lot of stuff and no place to put it. Books that wouldn't fit on the shelves. Framed posters leaning against the bookshelves because there was no room on the walls. A box of candles sitting next to the candlestick, waiting for a chance to burn. More vases than flowers. No place for an everyday object to hide, to take a breather from display. The place smelled of dog.

The dog. She trotted up to Manny, wagging her tail so hard that it made her head shake.

"Hello, Squeaky girl. Hello, little lady."

Squeaky girl was a brown and black mutt with gray hair around her eyes. I bet she was ten or eleven, which, after doing the math, would make her dead in human years. Walking around Manny, she lowered her butt every couple of steps and dripped some pee onto the floor, which was stained with the stuff. Manny tried to calm her down by firmly holding her sides, but Squeaky took this as encouragement and let loose heavier drops. Manny kept a roll of paper towels on the table by the door and quickly unrolled enough to blot ten pounds of bacon. Squeaky sniffed me and I made the mistake of petting her. (I remembered that Patrick had fallen to the ground to play with her. I liked dogs but wouldn't fall to the ground for any of them.) She circled me and walked between my legs and I lifted my legs when I felt there was a chance of pee hitting me. She was good, very good. Before I had a chance to lower my raised leg she'd douse the one that was planted, and sneakers just drink up urine.

"Oh shit. I'm sorry. Squeaky don't do that. Is it all over you?"

"A little bit. Hand me a paper towel."

"Well, she likes you."

"Does she only pee on people she likes?"

"No. She pees on everybody, but her tail's wagging."

"What's the problem with her?"

"It's some kind of bladder thing. The doctor said there's medication that can help, but I don't want to drug her. And she only does this when people are around. It's not like she goes all day while I'm at work. I got to take her out. Want to walk around the block?"

She got her name because she squeaked in the pound, when Manny picked her up six years ago, when Manny said enough is enough, she's an adult, had always wanted a dog, and now she lived away from her parents, who had always felt that dogs don't belong in the city.

Manny didn't seem drunk anymore. She asked if I wanted a beer, and I said yes. She said she could use a drink, as if she hadn't had four. But I didn't know what was going on in her head. All I knew is that her boyfriend was nowhere to be found, and, like cops, she had a right to as many belts as she could get her hands on.

She brought me my beer, and I sat on the couch, which had lost its spring. She'd made an orange drink for herself. Liked her booze colorful. She put a tape in a boom-box that was on a milk crate. I recognized the introduction to a Bowie song. Rebel Rebel. A great song. But after the introduction, after that amazing guitar riff, the song didn't continue. Instead, I heard classical music, an opera, a woman hitting outrageously high notes. Like a bird. And then it stopped. The chorus to Dylan's "A Hard Rain's Gonna Fall." Stop. More classical, this time a trumpet. Stop. A ten-second chunk of a jazz piano solo. Stop. A country harmony. Stop. More classical. That hallelujah stuff. I didn't know what to make of these medleys, and Manny knew it.

"This bug you?"

"Well, I mean, it's kind of hard. You get into one song and then, all of a sudden, something else comes on, and it's completely different. No, but it's fine. The beer's good."

"I get bored with whole songs, no matter what kind of music I listen to. So a couple of years ago, I put my favorite parts on a few tapes."

"But don't you kind of lose the mood, jumping from classical to rock and country?"

"I guess I could go that next step and make a classical tape and rock tape."

"Yeah."

"I've never heard anything I absolutely love as a whole."

"Nothing?"

"Maybe I'm just impatient. Thank God for technology." She patted the tape recorder. It had given her what she wanted. Like the dog.

"What do you do for a living?"

"I'm in the ad business."

"Cool."

"It's pretty boring, really."

"What do you do?"

"I write ads, copy."

"Anything I'd know?"

"You know Holt coffee?"

"Need a jolt, Holt?"

"Yeah."

"You did that?"

"It isn't Shakespeare, but it makes the point."

"What else?"

"Let's see. I just did one for the phone company. Let an old friend..."

"Bring old friends together. That's a good one."

She said there are a lot of dull spots in the ad business, sitting in on all these meetings, trying to figure out what rhymes with Holt or what image would appeal to old women who've lost their husbands but still like to go bowling.

On the coffee table was an herb log, about four inches

thick. She said that, according to some Indian religion, you're supposed to burn it when you move into a new home. It brings good luck. Her mother had given it to her when she moved in, but she'd never gotten around to lighting it. I suggested we light the log.

"Now?"

"Why not? Maybe it can still bring you some good luck."

"Okay."

She torched the baby, and it had wanted to be lit real bad, because it blew up into a big flame. Half of it was flaming, and Manny, maybe more frightened than she would have been without the colorful drinks, ran to the bathroom and threw it in the toilet. A wet herb-log floating in the toilet bowl. Squeaky was peeing everywhere because of the excitement. Hell, Manny could have put the torch under Squeaky and the dog would have dowsed it.

The buzzer buzzed and Manny jumped. I stood up, thinking the same thing. Patrick. He'd returned. Manny pressed the intercom button next to the door.

"Yes?"

"Ms. Mann?"

"Yes?"

"Ms. Mann, it's Detective Rizzi."

"Oh my God. Is something wrong? Has something happened? Did you find him?"

"No ma'am. Would you mind letting me in?"

"What? Oh, sure."

She held down the second button and looked at me, all the muscles in her face as tight as a golf ball.

"It'll be okay."

She opened the door for Rizzi. I couldn't read his face, whether he'd not told the truth on the intercom, and Patrick had been found. Dead. He greeted Manny and when he looked at me, just like at the station, I felt like he was accusing me of something. No bedside manner to this guy, making innocent folk feel like criminals.

"No, we haven't found him. I just thought I'd stop by on my way home to see if you'd heard from Mr. Henry. People have a way of showing up."

"I haven't heard from Patrick at all. There's been nothing."

Rizzi glanced around the apartment and sniffed.

"What's that smell?"

"Oh, it's just something my mother gave me. Long story."

Contraband? Maybe. Hmmmm.

"It's supposed to bless the apartment."

"Bless the apartment, huh?"

"So what are you going to do about Patrick?"

"I'll keep my eyes and ears open, Ms. Mann."

"Are you going to look for him?"

"We'll find him."

Manny was leaning against the hallway wall, blocking the entrance to the living room. She didn't want him there, didn't like his detective work, and she wasn't the type to kiss up, particularly to a guy who wasn't doing his job.

"Well, I'll be leaving now, Ms. Mann." He pulled up his giant sleeve to look at his watch. "I just wanted to touch base."

"Okay. Thanks. Is there anything I should do?"

"No. We'll stay in touch. Bye now."

The things Detective Rizzi might have been thinking when he left Manny's house that night. These guys are smoking something that isn't on the "allowed" list. This woman and this Lipkin guy are awfully tight for two people who've

73

known each other only for a day. There was alcohol on their breath. This doesn't feel right. In all my years as a cop, how often have my instincts been wrong? Well, don't answer that. But they're often right. Patrick Henry. Patrick Henry. "I gave you death and liberty." How does that go again? I'll have to ask the professor. "A country for a life." Who is this Lipkin character?

"You ever been in the joint?" a cop asks me.

"No, you?"

"Just for deliveries. Ever committed a crime?"

"Two-bit stuff."

"Jaywalking? Pot?"

"All of it, and more."

"You're pretty clean, ain't ya?"

"Yeah, but I've seen things."

"Not like me, you haven't."

"I bet."

"I've seen things that would make you puke."

"You ever puke?"

"Plenty of times. But it gets easier."

"The puking?"

"Na, just looking at things gets easier. Not the puking. You always get that scratchy throat and bad taste when you puke."

3

I could have stayed over at Manny's. She said the couch was comfortable, but it wasn't just the bad springs that made me leave. She was drunk, and things were moving fast for us friendship-wise, and I imagined her getting up in the middle of the night to go to the bathroom and freaking out that I, still a stranger in most ways, was stretched out in her living room, maybe snoring, maybe gripping a pillow between my legs.

She gave me her number and I gave her mine, and I said I'd call her in the morning. No, I'll be fine. I'll take the cross-town bus at 86th and head downtown. I've got a token, thanks. Good Squeaky. See ya, girl. Hey, watch the leg. Shit. Pass the paper towels. What? No, the sneakers will dry out.

When I hit the street, I told myself that the next day I'd ask Manny if she thought it was weird that I'd kind of latched onto her, or she onto me, or both of us onto each other. I'd say it was fine with me, this accelerated friendship, but if she thought it was funky, I'd back off, and we'd get to know each other at the normal pace.

At some point I'd have to tell Manny the truth about me, that I was sixteen, a runaway, that the only play I'd been in was an elementary school production of *A Christmas Carol*. Joshua Lipkin, a Jew, as the Ghost of Christmas Past.

Billy's mom said my father had called, screaming that I wouldn't be welcome at home until I apologized and went back to work. My mother was very upset, and how could I do that? Only an asshole would do that. Like baiting the hand-out man.

"Maybe you should call them, Josh."

"My mother is fine, well, as close as she ever gets. Don't let my father get to you."

"He doesn't. Not at all. I'm just concerned about you."

"I'll be okay, as long as I can stay with you for a little while."

"As long as you want. You know that."

Billy was sitting at the kitchen table, reading a book of math games written by Lewis Caroll, the *Alice in Wonderland* guy. I couldn't tell if he was stoned, but it was a safe bet.

"Any good?"

"It's pretty funny. The guy writes hilariously. I don't get most of it, but he comes up with some great lines, like 'No lambs are accustomed to smoke cigars.'"

I had no idea what Billy was talking about. I think it was the pot talking. It was getting harder and harder to talk to him. Depressing when you can't have a solid conversation with the guy you consider to be your only real friend. I hoped Manny would become a real friend.

I told them about Manny, how I'd finally met the woman I'd seen all over the city, and that she was looking for her boyfriend, who had the unfortunate name Patrick Henry.

"Patrick Henry?" Billy looked up from his math games. "The Revolutionary War guy?"

"Yeah."

"Give me liberty or give me death." Billy's mother remembered her history. "What do you mean, he's disappeared?"

I told her about their date, the spinning in Grand Army Plaza, the disappearance, the police, how Rizzi wore clothes that were too big for him, and, if that weren't enough, the guy couldn't get the historical quotes right. Billy's mom had a friend whose five-year-old had wandered out of Macy's lingerie department while the mother was looking at a price tag. A nice security guard calmed the girl down with one of the lollipops he kept in his pocket for situations like that, and eventually they tracked down the mother in cookware.

"How long has this Patrick been missing?"

"A couple of days."

"Jesus. And there's no sign of him anywhere?"

"Nope."

Billy had lost interest in his book.

"How long were they going out?"

"Ten months or something."

"Maybe he just needed some space. Ran away to think." Billy and I still thought alike. "You know the whole story, what was going on between them at the time?"

I told them the truth. The whole story was something I didn't have.

I went to see Jane the next morning. The attendants at Mayflower had broken out the party hats and were hanging streamers in the dining room for a celebration. Hilda Saltonstall, the sign said, had won Citizen of the Month honors, and this was the day for the gala lunch. Sadly, the only picture they had of Hilda — the one taped beneath her name — was an unflattering shot of a woman lying in bed, a grimace of pain on her face, her body partly blocked by one of those intravenous dripping bags. You'd think they could have found a nicer picture, one from when she was younger and fully capable of feeding herself, one where she showed her teeth because she was happy, not because her colon hurt.

It wasn't just Hilda who was having a rough time of it. Jane's door, like all the others, was open. Hospitals and nursing homes don't like closed doors, on the theory that you're less apt to die if everyone passing your room can peek in and watch you sit there eating and reading. I knocked as I entered and I knew immediately. A soft answer. Jane wasn't one hundred percent. She was in bed, with the covers pulled up so tightly under her neck that I knew someone else had done it, tucked her in. Her eyes lit up a little. And she smiled. But she looked tired, more tired than I'd ever seen her. I thought about a spent firecracker, a bullet that's been shot.

"Hey, what's going on? You okay?"

"Oh, I'm fine, just a little pooped. How are you, Joshua?"

"The doctor says you're fine?"

"He says the heart's slightly off, but that if I rest I'll be okay. Got a fag on you?"

"No, I don't. Sorry."

"You're lying to me Joshua."

"No, I'm not."

"I can tell when you're lying. You act nonchalant, too nonchalant, and you give it away." Hm. Not good for the Manny/acting/age thing.

"You probably shouldn't be smoking, Jane." She struggled to pull a hand from under the tight blanket, and she waved off my point.

"Let's split one, okay?"

"I don't know."

"Listen Josh. I'm 82 years old. If I want a cigarette, I should be able to have one."

"Okay. We'll split it."

I closed the door — DEATH! DEATH! — and put a towel on the floor at the base. I lit a Marlboro and we passed it back and forth. She didn't draw as much as she normally did, but there was still some impressive power in them lungs. I told her I'd left the apartment, my father, and didn't intend on going back, and she pulled me toward her and kissed my forehead. Her little-old-lady mustache tickled. And I told her about Manny, this woman I'd met at the library.

"See?"

"What?"

"It's good to be at the library, where the books are."

"I wasn't reading, Jane. I was just sitting there."

"You haven't been reading, have you?"

"No more than usual."

"And what's that?"

"Nothing."

"You're worse for me than this cigarette."

The cigarette seemed to lift her spirits. So did my telling her that there was a mystery attached to this library lady. Jane loved mysteries, read a couple of sleuth books a week. More important, she'd lived them, long before landing in Mayflower. Traveled to more than a hundred countries, more than I could name, and she always said the people and their customs, sometimes outrageous, were like clues she'd pick up in her international snooping. She'd seen three people murdered, all men, all not ten feet away from her when they were shot or knifed.

"I disappeared once."

"Where? Why?"

"It was soon after Lyle and I met and he was chasing me all over Europe."

"Chasing you?"

"Well maybe he wasn't chasing me, but it sure seemed like it. Wherever I turned up, he did. At this or that party, this or that city. I went to Paris, and he was there. Vienna, the same. Everywhere."

"Sounds like he lo-o-oved you, Jane."

"Well, I didn't lo-o-ove him. Not then, anyway. Feeling trapped is one thing you don't want when all you want is the freedom of traveling. You know what I mean?"

"I've been to Jersey. Yeah, I've traveled."

"Very funny."

"So you ran away."

"That's right. I went to where he couldn't follow me, unless he was in the same train. A place where no one knew me, and word wouldn't somehow get back to him."

"Where?"

"A tiny village in northern Italy. It was absolutely gorgeous, mountains and vineyards. The nicest people you'd ever want to meet. I gave this woman virtually nothing, maybe a quarter a day, and she put me up in her house with her family and fed me bowl after bowl of delectable risotto."

"Rice."

"You impress me, Joshua. Anyway, it was a couple of the nicest weeks I ever had, dealing only with new people and not feeling the threat that someone old, someone you know, is going to ruin it for you."

"So you completely dropped out of sight. I wonder if that's what Patrick did. I kind of think so."

"He might have."

"But you wouldn't have done that, what you did, if you knew someone was looking for you, I mean, if someone was worried about you, thought something might have happened to you."

"Such as after I was married?"

"Yeah."

"No, I never disappeared after I was married. Although sometimes the temptation was great."

I woke Manny up with my call. Her voice was higher-pitched than normal. She said she needed to take Squeaky out and then would have some breakfast. At some point, she was going to go and see her mother. She also wanted to do some woodworking. And there was Patrick to find. I asked her if she was hung over, if those colorful drinks had come back to haunt her. She said she never got hung over, just got hungry, and she was going to take care of that. I offered to take her out to breakfast, and she said that would be nice, but she preferred to eat breakfast at home because her apartment received good early-morning sun. She asked if I liked eggs. Who doesn't, I answered.

I knew Manny hadn't gotten out of bed, hadn't even looked out her window, because she would have noticed that the sun had become like Patrick — gone, vanished, bye bye — and so her apartment wouldn't be as lit up as she thought. Huge clouds blocked the sun, and the weatherman on Billy's television said it might thunderstorm or remain partly cloudy or partly sunny, whatever the difference is, or it could get completely sunny or completely cloudy. The guy covered all the bases.

Billy's mom knew someone who had disappeared. Jane had disappeared. This was my first exposure to the phenomenon. Maybe I'd led a sheltered life.

New Yorkers like certainty, hate it when the weatherman says it might be this and it might be that — with the this and that being miles apart. Mixed signals confuse them. Like a kid who's done something wrong, and the father smacks him, and then says, "you know I love you." Smack. "I love you." Smack. "I love you." What's a kid to do?

When the weather is all over the place, people get nervous, look up, like a cop glancing over his shoulder to make sure a gun isn't pointed his way.

I was six or seven. Genius Uncle Saul and my mother, long before vodka had replaced orange juice as the wake-up drink, took the cousins to the park for a game of touch football. It was on a day like this, and I actually thought the clouds were helpful because there was no sun to get in your eyes and keep you from catching that touchdown pass. But it started to rain, and we couldn't even finish the first half. We huddled under a tree and waited for the rain to let up. It didn't, and after an hour we had to make a run for it. A rain-run can make a kid giggly, but not if he remembers what could have been.

Even the guys selling bagels seemed down. No one wants a bagel if it's going to rain.

She was wearing jeans and a baggy T-shirt that probably belonged to Patrick. I looked forward, one day, to having a girlfriend I could share clothes with. Well, I wouldn't wear hers, but she'd be comfortable in mine, particularly my shirts, and that would be good. Manny's eyes were bloodshot and her hair was messy. She might not have had a hangover, but she was as close as you get.

I'd known her only two days and the black roots of her hair, in that short time, seemed to have grown out an inch. When you dye your hair, there comes a point when you have to make the decision to do it again or accept the return of your natural color. Manny needed to make that decision soon, because she was beginning to look like a punk rocker or a skunk, and she didn't strike me as either type.

She said she'd already called the police station. Rizzi wasn't in, but there'd been no news on Patrick. She'd talked to that detective whom Rizzi had called the professor, the one who knew everything about the American Revolution. He said, again, that these things take time. Most missing persons turn up okay. Manny wished the professor was on the case instead of Rizzi. The professor must have sensed this because he said Rizzi was top-notch, don't be fooled by the clothes and clownishness.

"Are you lucky, Josh?"

"What do you mean?"

"Do good things just happen to you out of nowhere?"

"No."

"Never been caught in a rainstorm of good things?"

"That your line?"

"Yeah."

"Pretty good, but no rainstorms. No."

"Funny thing is, I've always been lucky."

"Gotten wet a lot."

"Huh?"

"Rainstorms."

"Oh. No, I'm serious. I always won Bingo and the cakewalk. You know, when you stand on the right square and the music stops and you win the cake."

"I've never heard of a cakewalk. Where do they have 'em?"

"Schools mostly."

"Not mine."

"I've always won with chance."

"And now you think you're unlucky?"

"Not compared with someone who's had his legs blown off by a land mine, but yeah."

"Men and you, huh?"

"My first non-asshole in years, and God fucks with me."

"Must be really hard."

"A friend of mine, Mara, just had a baby."

"That's nice."

"It's great and she loves her husband and all that, and I can't feel anything but fucking bitterness and jealousy. I'm pissing myself off."

She made us breakfast. The bacon was crisp.

Manny's woodworking studio was in the basement of her building, next to the super's open-air office. He'd given her the space soon after she moved in, when she said she liked to work with wood, but her apartment was too small. All he needed was a desk where he could do some paper work, a spot to keep the keys, a place where he could escape to if the family got a little noisy and he needed a breather.

Jules was sitting at his desk when we walked in.

"Hi, Jules."

"Hey, Manny. How you doin'?"

"Good. Jules, this is Josh."

"Hey, Josh. Nice to meet you."

"You, too."

A huge, black man. I took him to be in his late fifties, but blacks age better than whites, so it was hard to say. His chest jutted out like a rooster's, though his voice was deep and soft, not a cockle-doodle-doo scream. His tight curls were going gray and there was a bald spot the shape of a shoe horn in the middle of his head. One of his teeth was gold-capped. He smiled a lot, more because he liked to smile, I thought, than to show off his jewelry. I doubt he ever showed off. Proud and quiet. If he ever played football, and guys that shape and size should, and if he ever scored a touchdown, I bet he didn't spike the ball or do a dance. Just walked to the sideline, thanking the guys for the opportunity to serve the team.

Behind Jules was his desk, a plank of wood laid over two file cabinets. A small radio. Probably liked to listen to the news or a baseball game. Silver keys, each corresponding to an apartment in the building, hung on the wall.

"I made Jules the nameplate for Christmas." He turned and picked it up from his desk. "JULES REED, SUPERINTENDENT," carved into a wood block. Jules was smiling bigger than before. I could almost make out some more gold, this time in one of the back molars.

"She sure knows her way with wood."

"Looks like it."

"Hey, Manny, any word on Patrick?"

"Nothing, Jules. Haven't heard a thing."

"Damn." He shook his head, thinking about Patrick, a good kid who seemed to make Manny happy. Jules walked over to Manny and put his arm around her. "Hang in there, baby. Everything will turn out fine. You just wait." He asked if we would excuse him, and, of course, we did, and he went back to his desk, where he began writing on a pink piece of paper. He wrote slowly, painfully, like it was a death order he was filling out, and not an order for a new lock, or door knob, or window pane.

She'd built shelves on two walls of the room, and there was wood lying on them, wood of all colors. Light brown and dark brown. Yellow. White. Some with green wavy lines and other with straight black lines. Some of the boards were long, maybe six feet, and on top of them sat little chunks, like the building blocks that I'd once made into a skyscraper that scraped my bedroom ceiling. Wide wood and narrow wood, thick and thin. The woman collected wood.

On the opposite wall she'd put up huge sheets of plywood and on them she hung her tools, files and hammers and screwdrivers and electric tools and planes and saws and chisels. Some were new. I could tell by how shiny they were and how few nicks were in them. And if they plugged in. But the majority were old, heavy looking things with dark wood handles and dents and scratches. They'd seen a lot more action than I had. Well, they were older than me. When I get to be that age, I'll probably look like them. Hopefully. Scarred but not so tired that I can't get the job done.

"My father left me most of these. I've bought a few. Whenever I find a nice old one, I pick it up. They really don't make them like this anymore. It sounds trite, but it's true." She pulled one of the bench planes off the wall. She cupped it in her left hand, as her right fingers ran over the cast iron bottom and the dark wooden handle. She asked me to feel it, to hold it. Some heavy tool. One blow to the head with this baby and you're gone. The handle fit my hand perfectly, or my hand fit the handle. I told her I thought it was a nice plane. If you work with wood, you want the tool to feel right. You don't want to be thinking how much more handsome the cabinet would look if only the tool matched your hand a little better.

A half-finished guitar was in the corner. I say half-finished, but I couldn't tell. It could have been a third finished, or two-fifths. But she said half, so there. Some of the frame was done, and you could see the insides, where the sides meet the back. The face was on the counter, ready to be put on, a pretty piece of wood, no thicker than a pamphlet, with green and yellow and rust-red wavy lines.

"Brazilian Rosewood. The best wood for guitars."

"Does it make a difference?"

"This stuff has the best sound. Listen." She held it in the air and tapped it with her finger. It sounded metallic. I didn't think you would want guitars to sound metallic, otherwise you'd make them out of tin, but I didn't know anything, and I had the feeling she did.

"It's nearly impossible to find this anywhere. My father always wanted to make a guitar and he got this wood just for it. But then he got sick. He put the wood in his will. Not that anybody else in the family would want it. It was just that important to him. The way someone else might put a car in his will, he put the Brazilian Rosewood."

"How much time have you put into it?"

"I don't know. Maybe 30 hours."

"How much longer before it's done?"

"Maybe another 30. Something like that. I'm going to try to do something funky with the fret board. I want to put some Mother of Pearl in there."

My father used to call it "Mother of Fucking Pearl" back in the button business. Manny's father was a carpenter.

"He did the woodwork in the lobbies of a lot of the fancy apartment buildings and hotels on the east side. He taught me everything I know, which isn't much, I guess. But it's something. To have a craft."

I didn't have a craft, or a skill, or an interest. I got the feeling Manny missed her father.

She said wood is one of those things where you can make something beautiful out of something that's dead.

The sun had won out, laughed away the clouds. Everyone in Central Park could jump and throw balls knowing that rain wouldn't upset the fun. That's where Manny and I walked, after we left the woodworking studio, after she'd told me that glue showing on the inside of a guitar is like the shadow of a finger showing on a photograph. A bad sign. You gotta be careful with the glue.

Squeaky came with us. She didn't pee much outside. I think she was too frightened. She'd gotten used to the wood floors and the couch. Couldn't curl up on the sidewalk and fall asleep.

Manny let me pick the destination. I asked if the ball fields would be all right, and she said she loved softball, particularly the way fat guys take their games so seriously. We sat on a bench, as Joe's Paint Supply went up against

West Side Plumbing and Heating.

I was going to come clean with Manny. The only thing I wouldn't tell her was my age. That truth would have scared her out of the park.

"I have something to confess."

"What?"

"I lied to you."

"About what?"

"I'm not an actor. I don't act at all. I was in a school play once, but that's it."

"Why'd you say you were an actor?"

"I don't know. I felt embarrassed that I don't do anything interesting."

"Well, you at least could have made up something more interesting, like being an astrophysicist or a circus clown. I mean, an actor in New York is nothing special." She was smiling. Everything was okay.

"I know, that's why I said it. I thought you wouldn't ask me too much about it."

"What's your real job then?"

"I said I work in a liquor store, and that's true. It's my father's place. But that's all I do. Nothing glamorous. Nothing that means anything."

"Listen. Advertising has less meaning than just about any other job. I get people to buy their jolts from Holt, and you get people to buy vodka. That's it. You really have nothing to be embarrassed about. There aren't too many jobs out there which really make a difference."

"Maybe."

"I have something to confess, too."

What could it be? It had to do with Patrick, I knew that. They'd had a fight that night, so it made sense that he'd split while she spun. She'd made up the whole disappearing act. There had never been a Patrick Henry, except for the one in history. Or the modern Patrick Henry really did exist, and she'd made him disappear. Killed him. She'd actually called the cops to cover her tracks. Amazing.

"Yeah?"

"I'm not really a woman."

My God, My God. Oh boy. Oh boy. Yikes. I looked into her face, and there wasn't a smile. Yes. Of course. She was a man. The low voice, the lumpy breasts (tissue paper or socks). She'd asked me if I was gay, not just out of curiosity, but because she was trying to pick me up. He was trying to pick me up. Patrick was his lover. If I looked close enough, I could make out the beard stubble that's a transvestite's worst enemy. Manny was a man. Even the name made sense. What to do. I felt like I'd just eaten cotton candy and someone was now telling me there was lye in them pink strands.

"Oh."

"What do you think?"

"Think? Think about what?"

"Am I convincing?"

"As a woman?"

"Yes."

"Very. I had no idea."

He started to laugh. A weird reaction, I thought. Then again, the world, as he'd just proven, was one weird place. The laugh was low at first and then it became loud and high-pitched, more woman-sounding than anything I'd heard from the women I'd known. The guy was good. Scary, sure. Worst thing was, Manny and I couldn't go on as we had before. I'd woken up.

So he put his hand on my knee as he was laughing, hysterically now, and I jumped up because I wasn't gay and the whole thing was getting creepy and, whoa, this person I'd taken for a woman was actually a man in drag. Squeaky, who'd been sleeping in front us, got up and peed on my shoe. A couple of players for Joe's Paint Supply looked over at me. If they only knew what was going on. Hell, they'd probably come over and beat the shit out of me, and do a worse job on Manny.

"I was kidding, Josh." Which meant that he was kidding about making a pass.

"No. It's okay. I'm sorry. It's just that I'm not gay."

"No. I was kidding about being a man. Jesus Christ. Can't you tell that I'm a woman?"

"What?"

"I was just fucking with you. I'm not a man. What, I look like a transvestite? That's insulting."

I was certainly being fucked with in some way, but I had no idea how deep it went. There seemed to be a lot of layers to this.

"You're not a transvestite?"

"No. I'm not going to take off my clothes and show you, but I'm not. Look, do I have an Adam's Apple."

"No."

"So there."

She didn't have an Adam's Apple, but I wasn't sure how rigid that rule was.

"I was just pretending."

It was true. I could see it. (Of course, I could see anything that someone wanted me to see. A gullible son of a bitch, me.) The stubble wasn't stubble, not a shadow of hair, but a shadow of the branch hanging down over us. She crossed her legs like a woman, and the calves were too

91

small for a man. Her fingers, long and strong, could only belong to a she. Manny was tall, but she didn't have the bulk of someone named Kyle or Dick.

"Jesus, you had me. I mean, not because you look like a transvestite or anything. I was just completely blown away."

"If you could have seen your face first when I told you, and then when I put my hand on your knee. That was the best. You got up in a hurry."

What do you do when you're in New York City and you're all bent out of shape because you've been taken in by a woman pretending to be a man pretending to be a woman? You buy her a hot dog. The hot dog guy wouldn't have been fooled by Manny. He liked her, it was obvious, and would have seen straight through the male masquerade. He didn't even look at me, the mustached bastard, even though I was the one holding the cash. Asked her if she wanted every topping known to man and didn't care that my meal would have gone bare if I hadn't pushed for mustard. A good businessman wouldn't ignore one customer while kissing another.

With the dog doing somersaults in my stomach, I decided to pursue the other conversation I'd wanted to have with Manny, before she'd claimed to have a penis.

"Can I ask you something seriously?"

"Seriously?"

"Yeah."

"You're a woman, right?"

"No, come on."

"Okay, what?"

"Does it bother you that I'm like hanging around you too much or something? Or not that. But, you know, because we've known each other for, what, only a couple of days, and I don't want you to think I'm weird or anything, but you know, you know what I'm saying?"

Amazingly, she did know what I was saying. She'd given it some thought the night before. No, she didn't have a problem. She liked to meet new people, would talk to strangers on the subway and on the bus. The difference here was that we'd gone beyond strangers, we were getting into some heavy-duty stuff, namely Patrick, and we were getting together outside of the place where we'd met. She only had a few friends, and hadn't seen much of them in the past few months, when she and Patrick had taken off like gangbusters. No one would become a good friend of hers without her approval. Don't worry. We're doing fine. She said I seemed like a guy without hang-ups. I was real, not overly self-conscious, she said.

"You think it's weird, Josh?"

"No. I'm having a great time. I just didn't want you to think I was some kind of creep or something."

"No, you're not a creep."

"Phew."

"I never liked to have too many friends, even in college, when it's pretty easy to spread yourself out too thin. I don't want to sound mean, but I feel it clutters my life if there are a lot of people around. Just a few friends, a few good friends is all I want."

"I agree."

"I got to go to my mother's tonight. You want to come, just for an hour or something? It's a great place."

"Sure."

"It's where I grew up. You can see all my stuffed animals, because my mother kept them."

I was becoming a good friend.

Manny's mother's apartment was the type that you see in movies about New York, so big you could actually see a movie in it, full-size screen, popcorn, and all. Tall ceilings and a long hallway that branched into four different directions. I think it covered half the floor of the building, and it was one of those mammoth buildings with gargoyles perched on the roofs, protecting the huge apartments from modern architects who would cut them into quarters or eighths, the size of Manny's place. It was neat, but not in the angry, tense way of my home. The carpets were worn, not frayed. The furniture, comfortable, used a lot, polished. On the walls were real paintings, nice ones, not posters behind glass or the pastels that suburban diners sell for $25, marked down.

It was an apartment where you felt welcome. I could have actually read a book there. No pets, particularly the loose-bladder type. Would have screwed things up.

The apartment impressed me first, and I still think about it when I enter someone's home for the first time, imagining and hoping that the inside is the same, that I've reentered it. But Mrs. Mann made a bigger dent. Before she'd started to shrink — she was in her mid-sixties, I guessed — she was Manny's height, and now she was a few inches shorter. It appeared that the shrinking had not been gradual but sudden, because the skin, particularly on her face, hung there, like it was shocked that its bone support had been so quickly removed.

A number of things made Mrs. Mann different. She wore jeans. Had thick, wavy gray hair with streaks of black. And it was long, down to her breasts, or the loose skin that had once been breasts. The only old women I'd seen with long hair were crazies in some of the bad nursing homes, where no one cares if you don't take care of yourself and they certainly won't do it for you. The hair was smooth on Mother Mann, not the scratchy forests you find on some nursing home heads.

Mostly, though, she was real smart, and not in the way of others her age. Old people who are smart usually talk too much. They got to get everything they know out in the open, because they might die tomorrow, and what a waste it is to die with spare knowledge in your head. Mother Mann knew a lot, you could tell by the things she said and by the seriousness in her eyes, but she held her breath, encouraged you to do the talking while she peppered you with questions. And answers. Shrewd and warm. Good qualities together. Like gum that stays sweet for a long time and stays loose enough for the bubbles to keep coming.

Manny had her small mouth. Had her nose, too. The eyes must have belonged to the dead father. There weren't many pictures of him around. One on the mantle above the fireplace, him caught by surprise as he was building some large wooden contraption. I remember thinking that Manny, even though she had some of her daddy's features, would end up looking like her mom.

After the introductions were made and the drinks poured, we sat down in the living room, under the high ceilings, in the comfortable chairs and couch.

"Manny tells me you two have just met."

"Yes ma'am. Just a couple of days ago."

"I met him in the public library, Mom."

"Really? What a fantastic building."

"I go there a lot. It's one of my favorites in the city."

"Except for the awful paintings in the McGraw Rotunda. Do you like those, Josh?"

"No way. They're big comic strips in my book. I'm just surprised. No one's ever brought them up with me before."

"A big mistake. Panel them over, I say."

"Cheers to it."

"Yes. Cheers. You too, Manny, come on now. Good. Now tell me, is there any word on Patrick?"

Manny told her. Neither the streets, nor the police, nor Patrick himself had spoken a word. Manny blew loudly out her small mouth. Frustration as much as sadness. Mother Mann shook her head and then gazed intensely at her daughter. It was like her eyes were muscles and she was flexing them.

"He'll turn up, darling."

"I hope so, Mom."

"Are you still in school, Josh?" Now, of course, she could have meant college or high school. I didn't think I could fool her.

"No, I work at my father's liquor store, on the east side. What about you?"

"I keep busy." Which, according to Manny, was her mother's way of avoiding talking about herself.

"You do more than keep busy, Mom. Jesus, you got to stop undervaluing yourself."

"I don't undervalue myself at all."

"Yes you do. She writes book reviews and a bridge column for the neighborhood weekly newspaper."

I asked if that's why Manny kept that bridge book with her.

"I've kept that book in my purse for five years. I read a page a week."

"She's always hated the game, Josh. In fact I think you hated all games, didn't you? I mean the organized sort, with rules."

"Most of them, yes."

"She always made up her own, and some of them were very clever. Then, when she was old enough, she started working with wood, with the tools that her father showed her how to use. She always had a talent with her hands."

The phone rang and Mother Mann excused herself. We could hear her clearly, as though she was plugged into our heads.

"Listen Mary, slow down. Okay, what? Yeah. Yeah. Jesus Christ, what an asshole. I told you he would be like this. The majority of men are assholes, and of those that aren't, the majority have a dark side that shows itself every now and then. No, I don't think Larry is really an asshole, he just has that dark side problem. Tell him if he has a problem with your volunteering three days a week, three days a week for Christ's sake, tell him to go to a psychiatrist. It's his problem not yours. Yes, that's what I'd say. She's here now. No, he hasn't turned up. Okay. I'll tell her. Bye."

I never considered myself an asshole or as having a dark side, but when mother Mann came back into the living room, I felt like a class-A schmuck.

"I'm sorry you two. Mary just needed to vent. Larry's just retired and he's driving her crazy. He thinks that because she wants to volunteer at the shelter three days a week, she's abandoning him. Now, back to you two. How's the guitar coming, Manny?"

"Fine. Good."

I asked when Manny started using that name instead of Tiffany.

When she was about 13, Manny said. Mother Mann said it was closer to 11. The name Tiffany, as anyone should have guessed, came from the jewelry store. The Manns had decided to call their daughter this long before the name became so popular, long before parents started experimenting with names, calling kids "California," in memory of a romantic honeymoon out west, or giving weird spellings to conventional names. Byll. Sallie. Jennifyr. Mr. Mann had blown the money from one of his east side paneling jobs on some diamond earrings for his wife, who was beyond joy, and when the baby was born three months later, well, mommy wanted to put all her joys in one basket and call them one thing. One name. Tiffany.

"She didn't seem to mind it at first."

"I never liked it."

"Then she became a tomboy, which was her father's doing, of course."

"I just didn't want to be named after a lamp."

"Something that can break so easily. She was a tough girl. Always beating up boys."

"Only if they started something."

"All these boys' mothers would call up and scream at me because my daughter had beaten the boys up. I actually got kind of a kick out of it. It was a nice role reversal."

She came home one day and announced that while she wouldn't legally change her name, she would from then on go by Manny.

"Her father loved the idea. He saw it as a sign of independence."

"What about you?"

"Well, I didn't like it at first. It was as though she hadn't accepted a present I had given to her."

"But you've returned presents to stores before, Mom."

"That's true. But a name is different. Still, I came around. The only time I'd call her Tiffany was when I was mad at her. But that changed after a while, too. She became Manny."

"And now look at all the Tiffanys running around the city, Mom."

"There are a lot."

"It's a good thing I go by another name. Otherwise I'd be confused with all the others."

"Oh, I don't think anybody would confuse you, Honey. One of a kind, isn't she Josh?"

"Yes, ma'am."

In Manny's room was the contraption that her father had been building when the photographer snapped him, a giant doll house that filled an entire wall, floor to tall ceiling, built around a real window that Papa Mann had cleverly turned into a miniature greenhouse. There were real plants, small ones, growing in the greenhouse. Manny said he'd made all the furniture, except for a few pieces that she had done when she was old enough to work with power tools. There were about 15 rooms, each with a wall of books, most with a fireplace. You got the feeling that the dolls led a fairly sleepy life, reading in front of a fire, nodding off.

"Where are the people?"

"My father tried to make some, but they never came out the way he wanted. And the kind you buy in the store are so cheap, or oversized. So, I ended up using my stuffed animals." The zoo was overflowing out of a trunk in a corner.

"When did he die?"

"My father?"

"Yeah."

"Twelve and a half years ago." I bet she knew the minute,

second, what the weather was like, what he was wearing.

"Of what?"

"Cancer."

The doorbell rang and Manny and I walked back into the living room. We heard Mother Mann greet someone at the door, and in walked a guy whose face resembled tree bark, with long and deep trenches covering his forehead and cheeks. He was Mother Mann's age, coming from a time when acne cream was a teenager's space-age fantasy, and the only thing you could do, at least according to my grandmother, was rub urine, particularly the first warm one of the morning, on the face. Maybe it wasn't acne. A war wound. Stumbled on one of those acne-making mines.

"Larry, this is Josh."

"Hello, Josh."

"Hi."

"Hello, Manny."

"Hi, Larry. Listen Mom, we have to go."

"Stay for a while, Honey, we're not going out for another hour or so."

"Josh and I are going to catch a movie." Which was news to me.

"Larry's a movie buff."

"Love 'em. What are you seeing?"

"Something by Bergman. I forget the title."

"He's a master. A cinematic genius. He uses the camera like a caress."

"Yeah, well we have to run. Bye, Larry. I'll talk to you tomorrow, Mom."

"Bye, Mrs. Mann. Thanks."

"Nice to meet you, Josh."

"Watch for the chiaroscuro influence." What a guy,

Larry, helping us with advice I didn't understand to get the most out of a movie we weren't going to see.

The second leg of the adventure started that night, when we were supposed to be in the movie theater, looking for the chiaroscuro influence. I'd gone to Billy's because Manny had said she had stuff to do, and didn't invite me, which was okay. All this socializing wore me down. Billy's mother was at work and Billy had solved a math problem he'd told me about, but he was stoned, didn't explain himself well, and I couldn't remember what he'd said before, so his ideas didn't fly over to me. We watched a music awards show. Some techie wizard, taking more time than he should have, thanked God three times. The Best New Artist of the Year didn't thank God once, but praised mom and dad for their years of patience and their understanding with her decision not to become a vet.

Then the phone rang. It was for me.

"Josh?"

"Yeah."

"It's Manny."

"Hi."

"I'm going to Cape Cod."

"What? Where?"

"Cape Cod. It's in Massachusetts. You want to go?"

"Why you going there?"

She'd gone to Patrick's apartment, looking for anything, and found a letter he'd started. It was addressed to a lawyer in Barnstable, which, Manny said, was a town on Cape Cod, the town where Patrick was raised. She read it to me.

Dear Bill: If the abutter wants to play hard ball, then I'll play hard ball. You wanted authorization from me to go ahead and dig into this job. You got it. I'm not going to be bullied around, particularly in my home town.

"What does it mean?"

"I have no idea. I don't think he finished it because it wasn't signed. He probably had more to say."

"I still don't see why you're going to Cape Cod."

"Maybe this had something to do with why he disappeared. I don't know. He could have gotten in over his head with something."

"You think someone might have gone after him or something?"

"Who knows? Patrick's parents are out there, too. I just called them up and told them what was going on. They're very upset. I said I was going to come out, and they thought that was a good idea. Patrick and I were supposed to go out there this week."

"Where's Cape Cod?"

"Haven't you heard of it?"

"Yeah, beaches and stuff. But where is it?"

"It's the southeastern tip of Massachusctts."

"When are you going?"

"Tomorrow."

"How?"

"I'm renting a car."

"You know how to drive?"

"Sort of. So, do you want to go?"

I did the math. (Some math I excelled at.) Except for my love of the city, I had nothing here. Cape Cod had beaches, and while I couldn't swim, I was hot and realized that a cold splash would feel good. And Cape Cod might have some answers to the Patrick puzzle. This wasn't just Manny's mystery anymore.

Billy said I was nuts, but he kind of admired me for it.

I wrote a short letter to Jane, telling her that I was embarking on the first travel adventure of my life, that she'd be proud of me, that maybe I'd write about it one day, like she had with her books. Then I got stoned with Billy and wrote a letter to my mother. I have it now. My father gave it to me because my mother kept it, and when she died, he thought I might want it.

Dear Mom:

I wanted to drop you a note so you wouldn't worry. I'm going to Massachusetts. I don't know how long I'll be gone. At least for a few days. You should stop drinking. Remember how you used to laugh? Maybe you drink because of Dad. I can understand that. That's why I'm going away, I guess. He's bad, and no one deserves to be around him. Maybe I'll call you while I'm away. I don't know. I'll be back soon. I think we all need to clean up our act.

Josh

4

I wanted a convertible. Fantasized about the sleek, black Batmobile. What I got, what we got, was a VW Rabbit the color of pea soup. Still, I hadn't been in a car in five years, since my father sold his Dodge Dart to buy a taffy-pulling machine (which he didn't know was broken) in a last-ditch effort to save the sinking candy store. And I hadn't been out of the city in three years, since we took the bus to Paterson for Thanksgiving with Cousin Ida, a claustrophobic who needed to keep her house windows open at all times, even in late November, even in a steady snow, so she wouldn't feel trapped.

The Rabbit ran smoother than the Dart. We were heading northeast, away from New Jersey and the frigid House of Ida. Manny was the type of driver you expect from a New Yorker who knows cars only from the back seats of cabs. Frightened. Excited. Incompetent. One mistake was getting a stick shift. Whenever Manny changed gears, the car jumped forward, throwing us within inches of the dashboard, even with our seat belts on. Poor Squeaky in the back. Manny had laid two arms-full of ratty towels on the seat, to give the dog a nice cushion and to protect the rental from urine-damage. But Squeaky was too sad to pee. She looked from window to window, unsure why the world was rushing by her so fast. She couldn't think of the fun of running on a beach, only of what she'd given up, the comforts of the past.

It took us a while to get out of the city. The traffic was bad, and Manny couldn't shift well enough to maneuver us into the faster lanes. We passed my father's liquor store. A special on cheap Spanish red. I could make out my father standing behind the counter, bagging a bottle, not even trying to smile. Customers pay for booze, he thought, not smiles.

When we hit the highway, we were both excited. Manny didn't have to use her left foot very much, and I could read the road atlas without feeling that the devil was squeezing my brain with one hand and my stomach with the other. We didn't find any of the natural beauty you expect on a road trip, just fast food joints and access roads with malls and drug stores and ugly signs so tall that you got the feeling they were meant for folks in planes. But if you're in a plane, it's not like you can make an impulse buy, pull over to pick up some floor tiles because the ones at home are peeling off and you just gotta have some new ones, now.

Manny was in a good mood. It would be a while before she started getting nervous about meeting Patrick's parents. And who could blame her for being nervous? She was supposed to be walking into the Henry house, arm in arm with Patrick, saying how nice it was finally to meet mom and dad, impressing them with her love for their son, reassuring them that his love was safe with her. Instead, she'd told them that Patrick had vanished, and she'd be walking into their panicked lives a stranger, and, worse, with another stranger, me. I didn't feel uncomfortable about meeting the Henrys. I was actually looking forward to it.

"Okay, Josh, You're my navigator. The only thing you have to remember is to give me a lot of warning when I have to change roads. I don't want to make any sudden moves."

"Sure."

"You want to listen to some music? I brought my boom box."

"Okay. You want me to put on the radio?"

"There's a tape in it. Just hit play."

A country song came on, a chorus about a guy who loved a woman who loved a soldier who died. Catchy. I started humming along with the tune and was beginning to bounce my head and slap the atlas when the song changed to classical, which didn't have a repetitive chorus. Then jazz, and so on. She let me turn the music down.

We drove by towns that I'd heard of. There was Mianus. You got to pity the folks who live there, what with the jokes.

New Haven, home of Yale University, where Genius Uncle Saul had studied for a time. He said Yale had been the place where he'd discovered that there were people as smart as he was. Kind of modest and arrogant at the same time. Manny said she thought about going to Yale, visited the place with Mother and Father Mann, but thought the city was a dump and agreed with her callous-handed papa that no school, no matter how good, could make the place livable. It's tough when you grow up in New York. Other cities are margarine to New York's butter.

New London, home of the Coast Guard Academy. That's where Billy's older brother, Jay, had gone after graduating from high school. He was a nice enough guy. Reminded me of my father, not in the sense of being nice, but because both weren't as talented as their brothers. Only Jay was the older brother. Must have been hard on him, cruising through life just fine until Billy comes along with his talents and makes Jay look bad. A younger brother is better able to take that stuff. Just look at my well-adjusted father. Handled Genius Uncle Saul like a champ.

Providence, another place with a good college. Billy thought about going there. I wondered what I was going to do after graduation. I had no interest in more school, college. Like I said, I didn't have much of an interest in anything. I was going to take the SATs soon, but I'd bomb them. So even if I applied, I wouldn't get into a good college. And if I got in somewhere, I couldn't afford to go, even though Genius Saul would probably help out. So I didn't have much of a future. But, more and more, I wanted a future. Billy had one. Manny had one. With or without Patrick, she'd be okay. I couldn't work for my father anymore. I couldn't wake up in my apartment, walk into the kitchen, have a stupid conversation with my drunk mother, and avoid smudging a spot cleaned by Daddy. I knew my life had to change. I knew why, just didn't know how.

"I called my brother last night," Manny said.

"I didn't know you had a brother."

"He's six years younger than me. He's a graduate student in entomology."

"What's that?"

"Bugs."

"Like an exterminator or something?"

"No. He's one of those guys you see on National Geographic specials, the ones who go to the Amazon and lie on the ground and collect insects."

"You get paid for that?"

"Well, you end up working for a university usually."

"Great job."

"Yeah. We're not very close."

"Probably because of the age difference."

"Yeah, it's true. By the time I moved out, he was still a kid. We never had a real friendship, like kid to kid or adult to adult."

"So what did you talk about?"

"I told him about Patrick disappearing."

"He didn't know?"

"No. We don't talk very much."

"What'd he say?"

"Jesus, he can piss me off. I said I'd been looking for him, taken some time off from work, and that I was going to the Cape to meet with the parents."

"Yeah?"

"And I mentioned the letter to the lawyer, how I thought it might mean something. He's an asshole. He said I sounded desperate. Do I sound desperate?"

"No. I'd look for my girlfriend if she disappeared."

"Exactly. I mean, what am I supposed to do, just say everything's fine and resume my normal life? He gave me the same line I've already heard from others."

"What's that?"

"That Patrick just needs some space. And if he finds out I'm looking for him, he'll just stay away, stay disappeared."

"You think there's anything to that?"

"It's bullshit. Ridiculous. My brother's just a fucking sexist. A woman looking for a man is desperate. A man looking for a woman is doing his duty as a man. Bullshit.

What if something has happened to him?"

She said she used to protect her brother from neighborhood thugs who would step on his ant and cockroach collections, who liked to hear the crackle under foot and see the teariness in his eyes.

"There was this one kid. God, I'll never forget him. He had the meanest sneer, and you didn't think it could get any worse, but it would when he stepped on Jason's bugs. This kid was the type who didn't want to grow up to be a baseball player or astronaut, but an executioner."

"What'd you do?"

"I whacked him. I'd use an instrument. I took a lot of music lessons and I'd hit him with my violin or clarinet."

"Jesus."

"I broke one of the buckles of my violin case on his head."

"Ow."

"You'd think that because I protected my brother, he wouldn't be such a sexist pig."

I'd never thought about sexism.

She started to cry, and every time she convulsed she pushed her foot down hard on the accelerator, so we were jerking back and forth, like the car itself was crying. I asked if she wanted me to drive. Did I know how? No. She was getting hungry anyway and needed to let Squeaky go to the bathroom, so we'd pull over.

We each ate a Big Mac, which is the highway equivalent of the Central Park hot dog.

I knew we were getting close to Cape Cod even before I saw the signs. Water to my right. It was getting cooler. That ocean breeze. I asked Manny where we were staying. She'd called the Chamber of Commerce and gotten the name of a small motel. She made reservations. It was cheap. Only 30 bucks per person per night. One room with two beds. No, I don't mind sharing a room. I'm concerned about money, too.

I'd counted my money before we left — three hundred Genius Uncle Saul dollars.

So, the motel wasn't what we were expecting. Who would expect a dump on the beachlands of Cape Cod? It wasn't overlooking water, it wasn't in a quiet sandy corner, it didn't have the sound of surf. The owner wasn't a salty, bearded pirate who said "arg" and walked with a cane.

Nope. It was called the Cape Cod Inn, but I wanted out. A dive on a commercial strip, wedged between a gas station and a Kentucky Fried Chicken. I couldn't understand the appeal. Where was the water? Where were the beaches? The owners were a husband and wife who were thin and angry and ugly, and kept a cigarette pack exactly between them on the counter. I wasn't around them long, but I knew, as well as I knew anything, that a second didn't go by when one of them wasn't smoking. "The owners," said the plastic sign on the wall, "welcome you." It was a small sign. Mr. and Mrs. Crosby might have welcomed us, but it wasn't as Squeaky did, with a wagging tail and a spitting bladder. No, the Crosbys looked at us the way a disease looks at a healthy spleen to be eaten. They could have been brother and sister, looked so much alike, behaved so much alike, scowled in sync. I didn't know what the marriage laws were on Cape Cod, whether bro and sis could have tied the knot. It wasn't a bad idea. Would have kept the Crosbys from fanning out, from hooking up with other folks. If I was a politician, the first thing I'd do is make a law forcing people like the Crosbys to marry each other and leave the rest of us alone.

We were lucky to beat the no-dog rule, which another sign, larger than the welcoming one, told us about. Our room was around the corner from the office, and we pulled up, out of sight of the smoking Crosbys, and I got out, opened the door, and waved Manny and Squeaky in. Manny laid the towels over the entire floor, just in case Squeaky got excited and leaked. But there was little chance of excitement. There were big yellow stains on the ceiling. Looked like my boyhood mattress, when I used to pee in my sleep. The bathroom had rusted out.

"Manny, I think we should spend as little time here as possible."

I went into the bathroom to put my bathing suit on under my clothes. Manny did the same. I wondered what her body was like. I'd find out soon, after we'd gone to the lawyer.

We asked the angry Crosbys whether they knew the lawyer, and they said "damn lawyers," didn't want to know any of 'em. It was damn lawyers — puff puff — who'd once tried to take the motel — puff puff — away from them, and they had to hire their own damn lawyer — puff puff — to fight it. We'd only be staying a couple of nights, we said. Yes, cash.

We drove down the scenic road. Big old houses everywhere. This was the good country, the type that succeeds in making the city look cramped and rushed and dirty. What you might call charm. Some of the houses were inns. I didn't think the Crosbys could look any worse. But they did.

The lawyer's office was in one of the old houses. The sign said, "Bill Richmond, Attorney at Law." Again, the country feel. But I expected more. Like the general store and the old men sitting around a table, smoking pipes, drinking coffee, telling war stories, telling the pesky juvenile delinquent, who wants nothing more than to stay there and listen to those stories, that his daddy will be coming to get him. There ain't too many places to hide in this town, the folks in the general store say. The country is big, they say, but it's also wide open, so you can find things.

The secretary was a sexy woman, no more than 20, who hung up the phone as soon as we walked in. Probably talking to her boyfriend, the fisherman, telling him that she didn't want to eat flounder again for dinner, because flounder gets boring after a while. She said Mr. Richmond was out, but would be returning soon. It didn't seem to bother her that we wanted to wait. She even got us some coffee. Richmond walked in about five minutes later. A young guy in a three-piece suit carrying a leather briefcase. His hair was short and his neck was thick. He kept his lips clamped together. Wonder how he ate.

"Can I help you?"

"My name is Manny, Tiffany Mann, and I'm wondering if I could talk to you about Patrick Henry."

The guy stiffened. His arms moved closer to his body. His neck grew an inch. It didn't seem possible, but his lips pressed against each other harder.

"Are you representing Mrs. Hornblower? I thought Peter Crane was her lawyer."

"He is." The secretary was all business now, liked to keep her boss informed.

"No, no. I'm not a lawyer. Neither of us are lawyers.

No, Patrick is my boyfriend, well, I hate that expression, I mean, what does it tell you, okay, so, for lack of a better expression, he's my boyfriend." Lawyers, I guessed, brought out the gobble-talk in Manny.

"Oh. Okay. Girlfriend, huh? You guys up from New York, where's Patrick?"

Where, indeed.

We walked into his office, and because Manny hadn't given my name and the lawyer hadn't asked it, I did the honors. Josh Lipkin. You, too, Bill. Just a friend. No, Manny's. Don't know him.

Manny told him about the disappearance, and he just nodded his head. I couldn't tell whether he didn't care or was just practicing the sympathy nod which they teach in law school.

He has to be somewhere. I mean, people don't just disappear. Have you called the police? Well, that's good. What'd they say? That might be true. God knows I sometimes need some space, from my wife, that is. He might not have had the guts to tell you. I'm sorry. I don't want to sound like a jerk. Shit, I wonder if something has happened. Did you call the morgue or something? Am I being morbid? His parents know? I like the father. Mother's kind of weird. Always tried to keep Patrick a little too close to her. Know what I mean? One of those over-protective types. But that's something else. Letter? What letter? Come on, let's take a drive. I want to show you something. Shelly, I'm going out for about half an hour. If Mrs. Steward calls, tell her the will's all done and she can pick it up. No, Potter's pleading guilty. We can take my car. You have a dog with you? Let's take your car.

Despite his degree, he wasn't an asshole. He sat in the

front. Manny jerked the car out of his driveway, and he gave directions. I sat in the back with Squeaky, who liked the company so much that she sprayed the seat. We'd forgotten to take some of the towels with us, and now the folks at the rental place would wonder what that smell was all about. I didn't tell Manny right away because she was totally focused on Bill's directions and she didn't know him well enough — like she knew me well enough? — to tell him to slow down, give her some warning, as she knew her way around a car, and around Cape Cod, about as well as he knew the IRT and the street maze of Soho.

We stopped three-quarters of the way down a dirt road, with woods to our right and the ocean directly in front of us. Bill led us into the woods about 30 feet, where the trees opened onto a pond. This was the kind of postcard beauty I'd imagined in the country. You could hear the ocean. Salt water and fresh water next to each other. All the fishes of the world could live here.

"This is what the letter's all about, Manny."

Patrick's parents had bought this land 10 years earlier. The hope was that their children, scattered throughout the northeast, would build houses here, a way for the family to stay centered. Patrick had been the first to make the move. Designed a home himself and had hired Bill to take care of the permitting, which can be a bitch, because the environment is real sensitive around here and you don't want to harm it if you can help it and there are people making sure you're on the up and up, building-wise. Everything had gone fine, until one of the neighbors started making a stink.

"An abutter?"

"Yeah, Mrs. Hornblower."

She owned the house on the other side of the pond, the

only house in sight, and when she heard that someone was going to build on her pond, and would enjoy watching the ducks swim on her pond, and might even throw a line into the water every now and then, competing with her grand-children for the perch and large-mouth bass of her pond, Mrs. Hornblower had a fit. Bill said she was one of those native Cape Codders whose ancestors had been on the Mayflower — I thought about Jane — and had been among the first families to colonize the Cape. She was a sour old granny who was living in the past, couldn't believe that the Cape had ballooned in population, that the open spaces were all getting built on, that there were stoplights and McDonald's everywhere you looked. I said she had a point about the fast-food joints. The area where we were staying didn't do much for the character of the place. Bill said they brought jobs and convenience, too. Some jobs, I thought, flipping hamburgers and breathing in fat all day. So, Hornblower was spending all her time trying to hold up Patrick's building, arguing before every town committee that the house would ruin everything worthwhile about Cape Cod. Recently, she'd gone so far as to argue Patrick's land was hers, had belonged to great grandpa Isaiah, that there'd been a mix-up with the deeds. Her protests were stupid and desperate, but they took time to handle. That was the ex-planation for the letter, giving Bill the go-ahead to continue with the Good Fight.

"But why would he write? Why wouldn't he call you?"

"I don't know. Maybe he was going to send me some other stuff, he's been sending me a lot of designs and things. Maybe he was going to stick the letter in."

"He didn't tell me about the house. He never said any-thing about it." This hurt Manny.

"That surprises me. How long have you and Patrick been seeing each other?"

"Ten months." I answered, which surprised them both, and made me feel weird. Why the hell would I answer?

"Yeah. Ten months."

"I'm sorry, Manny. I don't think this has anything to do with why Patrick has disappeared. No, it has nothing to do with Mrs. Hornblower. I can guarantee that."

A dead end. We'd hit a wall.

"Again, I'm sorry about all of this, Manny."

He asked Manny to keep him informed about Patrick and said that while we were here, we might as well enjoy ourselves a little. Gave us directions to a good beach, even though Manny was down and didn't seem up for splashing in the water. He shook her hand goodbye. Then mine. He was suspicious of me, I knew. Must have been the way I'd answered his question to Manny. Of course, he had a point, but I didn't deserve suspicion. You got to give an eager teenager a break.

I saw the scariest thing ever, but before that I saw Manny in a bikini. Now, it's always awkward seeing someone's body for the first time. At least when the situation is sexual, there's the anticipation, because something is going to happen to that body, there's going to be rubbing and kissing and all sorts of sweaty contact. It's understood that you're going to look, not peek but look, maybe even lick your lips, trying your best not to appear psychotic. But if you're talking beach, and the other person is just a friend, you know you can only peek, not stare, and you wonder if you're going to find that body attractive, which can be weird, or if it's going to disgust you, also weird.

Bad parts first. In the middle of Manny's cleavage — exactly in the middle, like the cigarette pack between the Crosbys — was a mole, a little brown hill, about a half-inch across. I was close enough to see that there weren't any hairs growing out of it. Thank God. I'd seen tons of hairy moles in nursing homes. Manny's wasn't that bad, but a mole's a mole, and it's about as pretty as New York City snow that's been on the streets for more than a minute.

The other problem had more to do with attitude. Manny was upset because the letter had been a bust and because Patrick had never come clean about his life plans, to come back to Cape Cod, with or without her, to the house that Hornblower hated. When she stood up to take her pants off she slumped, made dead weight of herself, and I bet even the most beautiful woman in the world can dim her beauty with a bowed head and collapsed arms and slightly bent knees.

But look. St. Patrick's has its sleeping bums. The library has the McGraw Rotunda. Central Park has litter. New York City has crime like there's no tomorrow. Nothing's perfect, which is another way of saying that, apart from the mole and the slumping, Manny had a great body. Found it hard to look away. Can't fight a magnet like that. Bigger breasts than I'd thought. A fleshy old butt sticking out in the other direction. Even if the mole had been hairy, the body would have still been a keeper.

I got an erection, so I turned on my stomach for a while.

Manny didn't seem to notice my body.

We'd walked passed the crowds to the edge of the beach. There were a few sailboats. I'd never been in one. The only people near us were a father and his two daughters. Twins. It was just this family and us.

I was trying to cheer Manny up, telling her that even though the letter hadn't worked out, it was important for her to see Patrick's parents. She was nervous. What if they thought, like some of the others she'd talked to, that she'd had something to do with it, driving him away and all?

"They wouldn't think that. Everybody can tell you're doing everything to find him."

"I hope so."

"They know about me, right?"

"Yeah, I told them."

"Did they mind I was coming?"

"No. I don't think so."

The two girls of the family were, I guessed, eight or nine, happy kids who worked well together, as all twins do, and had built a sand castle that was three feet high, with windows and crisp-line turrets that they'd carved out with a pencil.

Manny was on her back, eyes closed to the sun. Erection gone for the moment, I was sitting looking at Manny's breasts, then her stomach, then crotch, and the pubic hair sprouting from her inner thighs, then all the way down to her crossed feet.

We weren't aware that the family was swimming out too far. I looked up from Manny when I heard one of the girls say "Daddy". The voice wasn't loud, it wasn't a scream, but it was loaded with fear. The three of them were far apart. "Christine, are you okay?" "Daddy?" "Amy?" "Swim to the shore girls." "Daddy." The last "Daddy" was a yell, and both Manny and I stood up. The family seemed to be getting farther away, and the girls were on either side of their father, each at least 20 feet from him. "Help me Daddy." "Help me." Both of the girls were pleading now, and the one on the right went under water for a second and came up coughing and trying to talk at the same time. Then the other girl went down, and came back up the same way. Both of his girls were drowning, and the father had to go one way. He could only get the other after he'd gotten one. And I didn't think there was enough time.

"You know how to swim, Josh?"

She didn't either. She bolted down the beach, to get someone who could. She disappeared behind a dune. I thought I should have gone. I could sprint faster. I ran into the water, cold, till it came up to my neck, but still I was a long ways from the girls. They were going under more now. The father, telling them to calm down, hadn't moved much in either direction. Then the twin on the left let out a scream, which terrified me and must have done the biggest number on him. He swam toward her, frantically. He didn't seem like a good swimmer either. The other twin screamed. "Daddy, Daddy." He paused. But the only thing he could do was continue. Then come back. He had no choice but to choose. Twins. I yelled to the girl, the girl left alone. "You can do it. Swim to me. Calm down. Don't panic. Relax. Tread water."

The family was coming apart. The girl on the right, I knew, had seen that her father was swimming away from her. She stopped yelling, even as she bobbed up and down. The quiet dying. I'd known old people who were never calmer, never quieter, than right before their deaths. "Hey," I yelled. I couldn't see the girl's eyes, but her head turned to me, before it went under, and when she came back up, her head turned again toward me. "Swim to me. You can do it." "Help. I... can't... swim."

I jumped, and I lost the ocean floor. By paddling with my hands, I was able to stay afloat but I wasn't moving toward the girl, so I dove under water, actually I fell under water, and I kicked and kicked and kicked, and I waved my arms and when I emerged, I couldn't see anybody. I pivoted and saw that the girl was still far from me. The father had reached the other daughter. My girl was spending more time under water than above. Again I dove and pushed in her direction, and again I'd gone parallel to her. I tried to paddle, to catch my breath in order to go at her again. But I wasn't doing as well as before. I felt like my blood was lead and all of it had rushed to my feet. I went under.

Then something came at me, pushed me out of the water. A man. Told me to hang on. And he left. Toward the girl. I went under again. Someone else lifted me out by my shoulders, turned me on my back, and cradled my neck in the fold of an elbow. The most reassuring touch I'd ever felt. I breathed heavily and looked at the sun, which stung my eyes. But I wouldn't have traded that stinging, that pain, for anything. I could actually see the sun, high above the water.

A crowd had gathered on the beach. I was fine, I told someone. Help the girl. The girl. The twin who'd been saved by the father was standing with a towel around her, shivering, crying, dazed. She seemed both young and old. Manny hugged her, said everything was going to be okay. The father was kneeling beside his other daughter, whom a lifeguard was trying to resuscitate. Some ambulance guys rushed to her side, and the walls of the sand castle crumbled. One of the guys picked the girl up and ran her to the ambulance. The father, carrying the other girl, ran alongside. He was crying. The family was.

We drove back to the motel. Didn't have to deal with the Crosbys. Manny got us some Kentucky Fried Chicken. As I fell asleep, I saw the girl, only this time I was much closer. Her eyes were wide open and she didn't blink, even as she bobbed. She was mouthing the word "Daddy," but there was no sound. I could have sworn she smiled before she went down. Then I felt my neck in the fold of an elbow.

"I started swimming when I was two," the swimmer says to me.

"I never started."

"Ever swim against a rip tide?"

"No."

"You gotta fight for every inch."

"I bet."

"That's where the real swimmer comes through."

"You're a real swimmer."

"Sure am. You know, the problem with most folks is that they panic, and you can't get anything done when you're panicking."

"It's easy to panic when you're not used to something."

"I don't panic easily."

"If I dropped you in the middle of Harlem, a white boy like you, you'd panic."

"No way."

"I got five bucks says you would."

"You're on. I made five bucks baby-sitting last night."

We called the hospital before we left for the Henrys. We were inquiring about the twin. We didn't have her name.

She'd nearly drowned. Young girl. No, we're not relatives, but we were there when it happened. Tried to help her. Yeah, it was scary. Serious condition, what does that mean? And you don't know how long it'll be?

The shower woke me up a little, but I was still moving slowly and barely thinking. I stared at a knob on a drawer, a mirror frame, the wall outlet plugged up with cords from the television and radio. A cigarette helped, sparked my body, shook up my head, made me dizzy at first, but after I'd gotten used to it, it woke me up.

I'd brought a button-down shirt, and I put it on. Manny dressed up even more, chucking the jeans for chinos, and the T-shirt for a white, frilly blouse. You could see her bra. She brushed her hair back, saying that she was beginning to look like a skunk. My bathing suit was the only one that had gotten wet, and it hung in the bathroom.

Manny smoked also. Too bad they're so bad for you. You'd think all our brilliant scientists, you'd think Genius Uncle Saul, could come up with a healthy cigarette. Maybe a way to smoke our vegetables.

We left Squeaky inside after Manny had walked her behind the motel, away, we hoped, from the Crosbys' view. If the Crosbys got mad at us they'd do more than kick us out, more than force us to pay for the night. I bet they had their own dog, a Rottweiler named Hitler, and they'd sic Hitler on Squeaky and Squeaky's pee would anger Hitler even more than her mere existence and he'd pounce on her like the real guy had done on Poland, and Squeaky would give about the same resistance as the Poles. There'd be a newsreel about Squeaky rolling on her back and peeing in the air, while Hitler triumphed.

The Henry house wasn't far from the pond land where

Patrick intended to build the house that Hornblower hated and Manny knew nothing about. Instead of taking a left off the main scenic road, we took a right, and drove to the end, a dead end. There seemed to be a lot of dead ends on Cape Cod. It was a small, shingled house, looked old. There was work being done on the place. A dumpster right up against the house. One of those yellow digging machines. Scrap wood lying around. I didn't have much experience with home repair or remodeling, but I was smart enough to know the signs.

Mrs. Henry was at the door when we got out of the car. Of the folks who make a good first impression, most turn out to be nice, and some turn out to be assholes. Hello, Mrs. Henry. She was Manny's mother's age, but in every other way the opposite. There wasn't a hair out of place in the do of artificial curls. Beneath the hair was a tight, rubber-band face that had been in a few doctors' offices. Beneath that was a beige, polyester pant-suit. She held out her hands to Manny.

"Manny."

"It's nice to meet you, Mrs. Henry."

"Dorothy, please."

"Dorothy. This is a friend of mine, Josh Lipkin."

"Hello, Josh."

"Hello, Mrs. Henry."

The house was full of small porcelain animals. Dorothy heard me say "wow." She said she collected them. Elephants, kangaroos, bears, and chipmunks, all small and breakable and cartoon-cute. She probably bought the stuff mail order, falling for those late-night commercials that tell you only a limited number of Fuzzy the Cuddly Ferret are being made, hand painted, and you better get yours now because Fuzzy is a Favorite. I think half the world, including me, doubts that advertising works, that it actually gets people to buy things, and the other half, including Dorothy, proves that it does.

She apologized for the mess outside. They were putting a small addition on the house, and the place was upside down, and the workers were there every day, and while that was good, because they were working hard, she could hardly hear herself think and we should know what that's like because we're from New York, where they invented noise. Mr. Henry would be home any minute. He was out fishing. Sometimes he forgets that guests are coming over. Forgetful man. She asked if we wanted some white wine. Manny said that would be nice. I didn't like white wine, but this was Manny's show. That would be nice. Yes.

"Did you have a pleasant ride up from New York?"

"It was fine. It's beautiful out here. Neither of us has ever been out here before."

"Yes. Yes, it is. So, what can you tell me about Patrick?" She was still smiling, which was strange. There was no transition between the beauty talk and the Patrick talk.

Manny told her, and Dorothy nodded, occasionally sipping her wine and taking her eyes off Manny only when she wanted to check me out.

"And no one has heard from him, very odd."

"No one, Mrs. Henry. Dorothy. I've been everywhere. His store, the apartment, the places he likes to visit. I have no idea. I'm sorry I didn't call you earlier, but I thought he would turn up. I've talked to the police and they're looking into it, too. I came out here, we did, in part because there was this letter I found and I thought..."

"Yes. Bill Richmond told me." Small town.

"Oh, then you know that it didn't turn up anything. Maybe a part of me also thought that he'd come back here, back home, for some reason."

I said I thought that a lot of people who run away probably go where they feel some security, safety.

"Really?" Dorothy didn't seem to like me very much. "Would you like some cheese?" Manny and I took some. The mother seemed more angry than sad about her son's disappearance. That didn't make sense.

She was the type who likes to think that emotions can't get the better of her. She was stronger than emotions, wouldn't give into them. But her offer of cheese, like everything else about her, told you what she felt. You just wanted an honest statement. Not Camembert. A good cry. Not cheddar. A scream. Not brie. A "where's my boy?" Not blue cheese. Anything but blue cheese.

When the front door opened, everybody stood up. I could have been home, I jumped so fast. Mr. Henry walked into the living room. He was short, maybe five-five, with full blond hair and a big beard, and peculiar rubber boots that weren't satisfied ending at the calf, but rode up over his thighs, over his waist, up to his chest. The guy must have had a thing against water, I thought. And it wasn't even raining. Living on Cape Cod and fearing water. Damn shame. He said he'd be right back, and he was, minus the rubber.

"Hi. Greg Henry." Strong handshake. The introductions were made. He wasn't very affectionate with his wife. Patted her on the back rather than kissed her. He was the straight shooter of the two. Sorry I'm late. Tide was beating me a little. (Whatever that meant.) I'm going to make a drink. Either of you want something else...Yeah? Beer, Josh? Okay. (Dorothy smiled away my slight of her wine.) So, what's going on? Have you heard anything?

Manny spilled her guts, and Greg shook his head. It was bizarre, he said, that someone can disappear like that, in the middle of the city, while your girlfriend is doing a solo spin. He said he appreciated all Manny had done. And me, too. Manny said I'd been helpful. I didn't know their boy, but I knew Manny, and I wanted to help her. Dorothy sneered, like I said I been fuckin' Manny. Had to get Patrick boy out of the way. Got it, Mommo Henry? Baby? Had to move the boy along. If Greg was holding something back, like suspicion of me, he didn't show it. He said Patrick would show up. He knew it. He really knew it. "In the past..." He started to say something when Dorothy stood up and announced that dinner was ready. I'd never met folks like this.

Greg and Dorothy were both from Boston. They'd gotten married when he was working at an insurance company. She was the daughter of one of the company's head honchos. Greg was rising fast, not only because of the in-law in the corner office. No, he was good. But he was bored. The city, the big corporation, all of it suddenly lost whatever appeal it had once had. So they chucked it. Greg decided to move the family, now including baby Patrick, to Cape Cod. (I got the feeling it was mostly his decision. Dorothy smiled, but she never liked the transplant. Loved the city, the big corporation. Besides, wouldn't Daddy feel insulted?) Back then, Greg said, the Cape didn't have the junk you see now, the strip malls, the hideous motels, the fast food joints. Just open land giving way to ocean. You went to Main Street when you needed to shop. Dorothy liked the mall, said it was nice to be able to get things under one roof, didn't have to walk outside when it was cold or raining. That was the problem, Greg said, malls turning January into July, turning weather and nature upside down.

Greg worked for a small insurance company on the Cape for a while, but he was restless, felt unconnected with the place where he was living. So he started fishing, first on another guy's boat, bringing in cod and haddock. Then he got his own boat. And the money was pretty good, enough for a family that could keep a lid on its expenses, could live without going to a movie every night. Then he started shellfishing for clams and things called quahogs, big clams, he said. Liked this more, felt like he was farming, because you get into waders — those chest-high boots — and you harvest the ocean floor. Always wanted to be a farmer. At least he doesn't come home smelling of manure, Dorothy said.

I was chewing a piece of pork, Manny was sipping her wine, Greg was freeing up some bread crumbs that had gathered in his beard, and Squeaky was probably jumping on my motel bed and spraying my pillow with a yellow mist, when Dorothy asked Manny how long the relationship with Patrick had been going on.

"About ten months."

"That long?"

"Yes, why, you sound surprised?"

"Well, Patrick only told us about you a few weeks ago." The trip was not going well for Manny, and Dorothy, the bitch, seemed to take pleasure in my friend's disappointment. Dorothy might have thought she was hiding her feelings, but no sir. You just can't put a blanket over a pile of dog shit and say it's gone. I wasn't about to let Dorothy stick pins into Manny.

"Do you and Patrick talk a lot?"

"Not as much as we'd like of course, but we stay in

touch. He's our only son."

"We have three daughters, too."

"But Patrick's being in New York, I get worried, so it's important to talk, for my peace of mind."

"But in the past year, it seems he's grown apart from us."

"Greg!"

"What, Dorothy? All I'm saying is that he hasn't called very much, if at all, and whenever we call, he's always on his way out. I know he works hard, but I don't think he's that busy."

She began clearing the table, and Manny and I got up to help.

"We might not be as close as we used to be, but Greg is exaggerating, as he often does."

"I've only heard nice things about you from Patrick."

"That's nice of you to say, dear. I just wished we'd heard more about you." Zing.

While Dorothy prepared the dessert, Greg showed us, on Manny's request, Patrick's old bedroom. Aside from a couple of his paintings on the wall, a self-portrait and a landscape, there was nothing that said the room had once been occupied by anyone, much less a kid. Kids collect things and this room was bare, except for the basic furniture. Patrick's room had become a spare bedroom. Which I guess isn't unusual. After the kid leaves home, parents can safely box up junior's stuff and tell Aunt Mary or Cousin Pete that there's a clean, fresh, empty room to greet them on their extended stay. And there's no way the kid can feel un-loved. Life goes on. Still, I expected more from Patrick's room. I almost expected it to be like a dead kid's room, long after the death, with the parents unable to tear down the baseball banners, disassemble the erector-set bridge, empty the gum-ball machine, even remove a box of Lego from a dark corner of the closet.

We ate sponge cake with canned fruit on top. Good. Greg asked us how we met, and I told him. He seemed touched that Manny would walk the streets looking for his son and amused that two people could run into each other, or at least see each other, or at least one see the other, so often in such a big city. The other side of the coin, I thought, is people living next to each other and never knowing it, never seeing each other. A guy lives next to a woman for years, but he's always thought the apartment was vacant. Never heard a peep. Then he smells her. Been dead a few weeks. Cat's hungry. You get the picture. So he finally meets her when the cops remove her in the body bag, and he's never had a neighborly chat with her or borrowed a cup of sugar.

Dorothy asked what I did for a living, and I told her the truth. She nodded, smiled, and took a huge piece of cake into her mouth, all the while thinking I was a toad. I asked her what she did. She said she took care of the house and did some volunteer work for the church. Greg asked about Manny.

"I write ads."

"Commercials, you mean?"

"Yes, for television."

"Well, Dorothy loves television."

"I do not."

"Yes you do, Dorothy, you watch it all the time."

"I watch some shows, but I don't know anything about commercials."

"Don't listen to her Manny, she certainly does know

something about commercials. She's always singing those jingles."

"I am not, Greg."

"How does that soap one go?"

He started to sing, and Manny and I chuckled. Dorothy made a mental note to cut off Greg's penis later. A silence followed, so everybody took a bite or sip. Dorothy was ready to say something, but Greg beat her.

"You know, Patrick has disappeared before." Bang. "What?"

The bombshell. Dorothy shot out of her chair and walked into the kitchen. Between a walk and a run. "Can I see you, Gregory, please? Now."

He looked at Manny and bit his lower lip. Coward. He followed his wife. I asked Manny, in a whisper, if she knew what was happening.

"I have no idea. What the hell did he mean by that?"

"Beats me."

"Jesus, I feel like smashing some of her animals."

"I know what you mean. She's a bitch."

"First class. With a mother like that it's amazing that Patrick is so nice to women."

The Henrys returned, Dorothy leading her husband and smiling insincerely and returning a strand of hair to its assigned curl.

"Excuse us, Manny and Josh. I'm sorry. I think I'm just overwrought. Will you please forgive us? It's hard. Well, you know."

"What did you mean when you said that Patrick had disappeared, Greg? Anything you can say will help me."

"What he meant, Manny dear, is nothing. He was talking about something a long time ago, when Patrick was a

130

child."

"What happened?"

"Oh, he just ran away one day because we all got into a fight. I don't even remember what it was about. But that was when he was a child, and children run away over the silliest things. He's a grown-up now, so I don't even know why Greg brought it up."

Greg was looking down at his empty dessert plate. He didn't buy what Dorothy was saying. It was obvious.

"I spoke out of place, Manny. I'm sorry. That was a long time ago. Dorothy is right. Sorry."

Cape Cod. What a beautiful spit of land, what a gorgeous ramp to water. A place that raised your hopes in a few words, and shot them down just as fast. Couldn't advertise that in the Chamber of Commerce brochure, but it was there, as real as the mole on Manny's cleavage or my dislike for Dorothy. If Manny weren't in the picture, if we didn't need to keep up appearances, and I just ran into Dorothy on the street, and she started putting on a show like this, I'd tell her, point blank, that she reminded me of my asshole on a bad day.

"Would either of you care for an after-dinner drink? Manny? Cognac, Schnapps?"

The doorbell rang. Thank God. It stopped the conversation, which was headed downhill, even when it seemed it couldn't drop any farther. Dorothy left us, and Greg, quiet, refused to make eye contact. A loud, happy, Santa Claus voice filled the room and, I bet, the entire neighborhood. Dorothy led him in. A big old man with a red and white swirling face, like ketchup laced with mayonnaise. He held a cap in his hand. Had a few white toothpicks of hair, shaved to a half-inch long. He wore a white dress shirt and plaid pants, with colors that should never be seen in the same room, much less on one article of clothing. Green. Red. Purple. Blue. Yellow.

Everything about him was big, his feet, his nose, his mouth. He looked like a drinker. I'd seen that type of swirling face hundreds of times in the liquor store. My father made a lot of his money on swirling faces. But those folks looked like they would swirl into death at any time, and this guy seemed real healthy, as far from heaven or hell as I was, and I didn't see myself kicking off any time soon.

"Look who's here Greg, what a nice surprise, isn't it?"

Greg brushed off his shame and returned to life. "Damn good to see you, Francis."

"Damn's the right word, Gregory. Hot as hellfire. I had to change shirts three times today. Well, who've we got here?"

Dorothy introduced us. Francis Gallagher seemed as interested in me as in Manny, even though she was the one with the family connection. Maybe it was because I was a man, or nearly, and he was one of those old-timers who naturally prefers guys, particularly when the woman looks like one of those modern types that don't take no shit. He took a packet of peanut butter crackers from his shirt pocket.

"Anybody want some of these? No? Boy, these are good. Never had 'em when I was a kid, but now I go everywhere with 'em, movies, out walking, just sitting at home. Doc even says they're good for me. I asked him just the other day why this peanut butter tastes so much better than regular peanuts. And I don't even like peanuts. He didn't know. Guy knows a lot, but not that."

"Would you like a drink, Francis?"

"Dorothy, nothing washes down peanut butter crackers

as well as a little whisky."

He knew all about Patrick, asked Manny to walk him through the night of the disappearance.

"Spinning?"

"Yeah, we always danced outside the Plaza."

"The Plaza, huh? That's an expensive place."

"We'd just go there for a drink."

"Nothing wrong with a drink every now and then. You got to watch it though, don't you?"

"If you have a problem, I guess."

"So, you stopped spinning and Patrick was gone."

"Yes."

"And you looked all over the place, and he was nowhere to be found."

"Yes, that's right."

"You two been together long?"

"What, me and Josh?"

"Oh, I'm sorry. Are you two together now?"

"No, not at all. You looked over at Josh, so I didn't know what you meant."

"I was talking about Patrick."

"About ten months."

"Things been going well? Any problems?"

"No, everything's fine. Why are you asking me all these questions?"

I asked him if he was a cop.

"You're a sharp boy, ain't ya?"

Retired Boston cop. Had been on the force for 31 years. Sergeant. "How about another whisky, Dorothy? Boy, this peanut butter sticks in your mouth." He'd lived in the South End with his wife, God bless her soul, on the same street as Gregory's family. Was close friends with Gregory's father, had watched little Greg grow up to be a fine young man. Thought of Patrick as a grandchild. No kids of his own. Leanne, God bless her soul, couldn't have any, wanted 'em like nothing else. She lived an honest life, Lord knows, and was a happy woman, but passed away with an emptiness in her. They saw the Henrys as their extended family. Leanne died a couple of years after Gregory moved his brood to the Cape. When Francis left the force, there was nothing keeping him in Boston, so he came out here, nearer to his adopted family. "You're blushing, Gregory. Always a sensitive boy." Anyway, he thought he'd pick up golf on the Cape, join all the other silver-haired folks. He liked the game. It was like a walk in the park. And, even though he was getting up there, the game made him feel strong, because he could hit the dimpled ball a mile.

"You like golf, Josh?"

"Never played. I'm not a big sports fan."

"And what do you do for a living?"

"I work in my father's business."

"What's that?"

"A liquor store."

"Jesus, you hardly look old enough to drink."

"What about you? You're completely retired?"

"Well, I keep busy. People call me up to look into things, help them somehow."

"A private investigator?"

"Yeah, I guess you could say that."

He apologized if we thought he was grilling us. Old habit, but he didn't mean anything personal by it. Just wanted to get to the bottom of it. Dorothy had called him up, to see if he could lend his expertise. He wanted to work with Manny and me, not against us. He was just an old Boston cop who was used to dealing with these things heavy-handedly. The stories he could tell. Manny told him about the letter to Bill Richmond and how we'd pinned our hopes on it.

"You thought Hornblower might have something do with Patrick disappearing?"

"At first, yeah."

"Gloria's the last person who'd want to see Patrick out of the picture. Oh, excuse me, Dorothy. No, Gloria lives for the fight, and she'd like to see a fight go on as long as possible. These things keep her alive, I think. If she didn't have anyone to fight, if she was told that she could calm down and just play with her grandchildren for a change, she wouldn't know what to do. No, the only thing she ever wants for Christmas is someone to take to court."

Even though he came on heavy, I liked him. He sure put Hornblower in her place. And he was different from Dorothy. Seemed like a real human, someone who might keep secrets, but wasn't driven by them. And different from Greg, too. Seemed strong. You got to watch the sauce, he'd said to Manny. In less than half an hour, he'd downed three whiskies. Dorothy knew to bring him the bottle.

I wasn't down on booze just because my mother had taken that wrecking ball to the head. At some point you have to forget the wrecking ball itself and try to figure out why the person is so screwed up that she points to her forehead and says, "give me your best shot, right here."

"So, what do you folks think of the Crosbys?"

It didn't occur to me to wonder how Francis knew where we were staying. We hadn't talked about it with the Henrys.

"It's pretty dingy."

"What about you, Manny?...Manny?"

135

"Oh, I'm sorry. I was just thinking about what Greg had said, that Patrick had disappeared before."

Francis looked at Dorothy and Dorothy looked at Greg and Greg looked at the invisible air covering the tablecloth.

"I didn't know you'd gotten into that. But listen, kids, that was a long time ago. It's not relevant. What we have to do is focus on where Patrick is now. You think the motel is a little dingy, too, do you Manny?"

"What? Yeah, it's bad."

"I have an idea then. Why don't you two stay with me, starting tomorrow, cause it's getting a little late now? What do you say, Manny?"

"We'll be fine, thank you. We don't want to inconvenience you."

"Inconvenience me? Not a chance. I'd love the company. And it would be good to get you out of the motel. The Crosbys aren't bad people, but they're not all together, you know, in the head. So, what do you say?"

"But we're only staying another day or so."

"What kind of host wouldn't be grateful for that? Just kidding. It would be my pleasure, okay?"

"It's fine with me. Josh?"

I knew something was going on. I didn't know what. Like a meal that's got a spice you can't figure out. Francis. Patrick disappearing before.

The Crosby Man was standing outside the motel office when we pulled in, so we couldn't avoid talking to him, or at least greeting him. He didn't say hello. Just smoked his butt and scowled and said this to us.

"Don't like troublemakers."

What was going on in the little brain of Crosby? Maybe he thought we were lawyers investigating complaints that he'd married his sister. Not that anybody in his right mind would have complained about that.

Squeaky had peed on the towels. Strange. Nothing had happened to the room that would have excited her. Or so we thought. Manny took her out, but the bladder wouldn't give any more. We'd forgotten to tell Francis that we traveled with a dog. She called him.

"That's weird," she said to me.

"What?"

"I told him about Squeaky, and he said 'yeah' like he already knew about her."

"So it's okay?"

"Yup. He said he has his own dog who'd love a playmate."

Manny had brought her father's small toolbox and some of the thin pieces of wood that would one day form the Manny Guitar Masterpiece. I had no doubt it would be a masterpiece. She set herself up in the corner of the room and took a bench plane to a piece of spruce for the instrument's neck. As she carved her tree — she seemed more content than I'd ever seen her, in the few days I'd known her — I sat in front of the television, opting for a game show instead of a movie about a boy who confesses his love for a girl one day before doctors determine that his internal organs are so mangled that it's amazing he's lived this long, and he shouldn't make any long-term plans. The TV guy asked a question about German history. The contestant scratched his head. But Manny knew. "Bismarck." Question about literature. "Faulkner." She could do a lot of things at the same time. Question about science. "Kelvin." About art. "The Night Watch." "Montana." "IBM." "Tangent." "Lake Ontario." "Four." She got every one right. I thought, maybe I should go to college after all. Jane would be proud. Would have been proud.

Tired, I laid down on my bed, intending to creep under the covers in a little while and sneak off my pants. I hadn't had pajamas since I was a kid. I would get some in New York, for occasions like this, when you're asked to sleep in the same room with a woman you're not sleeping with. Manny came out of the bathroom wearing an opaque nightgown, starting at her neck and ending below her knees. It left everything to the imagination. But I'd never had a problem with my imagination.

There was a peanut butter cracker on the floor next to my bed. I held it in my hand. I told Manny. No, she hadn't brought any from the city or taken some from Francis, one of them somehow ending up in her pants and somehow ending up on the motel floor. Yes, Francis had been here. That's why Squeaky had peed. Francis made the mistake of petting her, maybe worried she was some kind of guard dog and tried to calm her down. I didn't know when he'd come. Who knows what he was looking for. The guy was sloppy, though, not covering up his tracks. We'd ask him about it tomorrow. No, I thought we should still go to his house.

"Anything to escape this place. We have to convince this guy that he's all wrong. He's looking in the wrong place. Maybe Dorothy's putting thoughts into his head."

"And where does she get the thoughts from?"

"I don't know. Bad thoughts have to start somewhere."

Dorothy seemed a likely place.

We'd been asleep one hour or two when Manny started

talking, softly at first, but then louder. "What Pat? Oh, my plane. My plane. My plane! Plane! Fuck you! Fuck you! I got you now. I think so. I think so." It's a good thing she didn't repeat herself so much when she was awake because I'd have to cork her annoying mouth. And she probably wouldn't have had much success professionally, pitching advertising ideas to clients. "This is my proposal, Mr. Holt. This is my proposal, Mr. Holt. It'll work. It'll work. What? What? Am I repeating myself? Am I repeating myself? Sorry. Sorry."

The talk turned to mumbling and I began to slip back into sleep, but then she started to cry. I opened my eyes and squirmed. She wasn't awake. To make sure, I said her name. "Manny, Manny, you okay?" No answer. I put my pants on under the covers, got out of bed, and walked over to her. "Hey, Manny." She was on her side, and a little puddle of phlegm had formed under her nose. I touched her shoulder. I sat down. I shook her. "Manny, wake up. Manny, wake up." I was beginning to repeat myself, too. Her crying was getting more fluid sounding, and I could have worried abut her drowning in the phlegm. But it wasn't that. I shook her again, and she shot up, hitting my chin. I bit my tongue.

"Oh God, what's happening?"

"You were dreaming."

"I know."

"And crying."

"It was so sad. Jesus."

"What? Do you want to tell me?"

"So sad." And, as if the dream hadn't done enough damage when she was asleep, now, with her eyes half-open and her body upright, she cried all over again.

"What's going on, Manny?"

"Everything's all fucked up."

"It's not that bad."

"Can you hold me?"

"What?"

"Please hold me." I'd never been asked to hold anyone. That's what you get when you grow up in a family like mine, where touching means a smack across your head because you've allowed a vacuum plug to fall out of its outlet. But this was Manny, the first woman, the first person, I'd not wanted to be away from. I held her, and after a few seconds she wanted to lie down. I moved to get up, but she told me not to stop holding her. She was under the covers. I was on top of them. She faced away from me and I faced her. She fell asleep fast. It took me a while because her butt was pressed up against me, or I was pressed up to it. That night, interestingly, I dreamed about Gina. Her face was fuzzy, as it should have been. Gina's face was turning into Manny's.

"Are you screwed up?" a psychologist might ask me, if I told him about the way my life used to be.

"You're not too subtle, are you?" I'd answer.

"I don't give a damn about subtlety."

"I have some problems, sure, but it's not that bad."

"Ever had a homosexual experience?"

"No."

"Ever want to?"

"No."

"Ever had any sexual experience?"

"That's an interesting question."

Manny

"You're a lying sack of shit."
"I am not. Why are you being like this?"
"I see confrontation as a tool, asshole."

5

I had no idea what made the Crosbys happy, but, boy, they came as close as I'd imagined they could get when we walked into their office and told them we were leaving. They nodded and exhaled together. Didn't need to smile, probably couldn't. But the mood didn't last. Through a cloud of smoke that momentarily blocked both of their faces (which wasn't a bad thing), Brother Crosby spoke.

"Can you read?" This wasn't a kind question, like he was asking for help because the Motel Licensing Bureau had sent them a questionnaire concerning the h-o-s-p-i-t-a-l-i-t-y i-n-d-u-s-t-r-y on Cape Cod, and he was embarrassed that the tough words were licking him. No, it was mean. But we'd paid. We had nothing to lose. And I can be a courageous son of a bitch when I have nothing to lose.

"Yes, how about you?"

"Can you read that sign?" He pointed behind him.

"You mean the one about the owners welcoming us. Yeah, I can read it, but I haven't felt very welcome, I'll tell you that. I mean, you haven't offered me one of your cigarettes, you haven't invited me into the back room. It's like

142

I'm a stranger or something. What gives, Crosby?"

"The dog sign, pal. The dog sign."

"Yeah, Crosby, I got that sign, I own that sign. What's it to you?"

"I seen your dog."

"What dog?"

"Your dog."

"My dog?"

"Or hers. I don't know whose. But it's a dog. And that's against the rules."

"That's not a dog, Crosby. That's a ferret. His name's Fuzzy the Cuddly Ferret, and he's the best fucking animal I've ever had."

"It's a dog."

"It's not a dog, Crosby. It's a ferret, and I don't see a sign telling me I can't bring a ferret in here."

"Get out of here, now, both of you."

"Not so fast, Crosby. I own this joint now."

"What are you talking about?"

"I'm a lawyer, undercover. That's right, a lawyer. I got degrees coming out my ass. And tomorrow, one of my deputies will be giving you my...my habeas corpus. So you can kiss this motel goodbye." I pointed to Sister Crosby. "You can stay on, Sweetie, just 'cause you're so goddamned gorgeous. You got me all hard, right now, just looking at you."

I winked and we ran and the car started and we drove away. The click I heard as we sailed down the street might have been the radio being turned on, might have been Brother Crosby cocking a gun he'd named Honey.

They got to make hospitals nicer. I know it's a place where people die, but it's also a place where babies are born, where lucky folks make miraculous recoveries. They should paint the walls pink, pipe in some Burl Ives Christmas music, hire comedians to walk the halls. Good practice for the night-clubs. But this is something for the future, like smoking your vegetables.

Some people are afraid of the dark, but a hospital can make you afraid of the light. I was okay, kept in a good mood by the way I'd handled Crosby and because I wasn't a patient in a bed facing a cinder block wall painted white. I didn't have a disease. I had pains every now and then, sure, those lightning stabs to the heart that scare you but then go away and you realize it's just part of being alive, being constantly reminded of death. But the hospital folks don't have it so easy. Their pains don't go away, aren't re-minders. They can only look at the white walls and the fluo-rescent lights and wonder when all this brightness will end.

Manny didn't do as well. She walked stiffly through the entrance doors and continued that way through the halls, around the inactive machines, around the patients on roll-ing beds who were either waiting for a trip to the operating room or waiting for an attendant to take them on a hospital joyride, perhaps their last. She said hospitals gave her the creeps. First there had been her uncle, her father's brother, who was sick with cancer. She remembered how the treat-ment had tanned his skin. If he'd been on a beach, he would have fit right in. Except for the bald head. And the moan-ing. And coughing. Manny was 15 at the time, liked her uncle, but didn't know him well, was sad because her father cried every day for two weeks, and she'd never heard that sound from him before, and it was so freaky that she had to plug her ears.

Then it happened to Papa Mann, the same thing, the cancer took the same path, and the treatment brought out the hair and the same false-healthy glow. And, again, she plugged her ears as her father coughed and as her mother cried by his hospital bed, and the plugging made her own sobs louder. She'd come to the hospital every day, talk to the doctors, who said, for a while, that there was a chance. When the doctors started shaking their heads or gripping her shoulders and telling her to hang in there, she started missing visits. Four times a week, then three, then two. Her mother didn't say anything. She must have known how hard it was for her daughter. Manny would walk the streets, but she couldn't turn a corner without seeing her father in her head, and she didn't know if this was any better than actually being there. She couldn't be there. She visited him on a Wednesday, and his eyes were closed. She told him that she loved him. He died the next day, when she was walking the streets, seeing him in her head. She didn't know whether the "I love you" line had done him any good. It hadn't done shit for her.

I asked her if she was worried about cancer because, you know, these things swipe at families, everyone. Yes.

We took the elevator up to the second floor, where the twin was. June. Her name was June. We walked down the hall, and about 20 feet from us, sitting on a bench, was the father, hugging what I guessed was his wife. Manny and I stopped. We couldn't tell if they'd heard anything or if they were just waiting, hugging the time away, because there's not much else you can do. Manny took my hand. We walked a few steps closer. The father looked up from his wife's head.

He didn't think we were strangers. He stared at us too long. But he didn't seem to know us either. He lowered his head into his wife's hair. They could have been tired, I thought. We turned around, took the elevator down, and got out of the hospital, into the air.

Manny was thinking of her father as she drove us away. She wasn't concentrating on the Rabbit, and we stalled at every light. I wondered how our relationship would have been different if I'd come into her life when she was happy. If Patrick hadn't disappeared. Of course, if Patrick was still in her life, dating her and helping those spins in Grand Army Plaza, she wouldn't have had time or need for me. No lying next to her at night, pressed up against her. No holding hands in the hospital. I'd be just another friend, and that would be the best scenario. Another piece of furniture in her cluttered apartment. For the first time, I was grateful that Patrick Boy wasn't in the picture.

On our way to the Francis house, we hit a little village center, with a Main Street that Manny said was vintage New England. Antique shops and T-shirt shops. Little men and women, the owners, sitting under little awnings, getting some shade and saying hello to passers-by, not seeming to care if people walked inside and, God forbid, bought something. The Jews of 47th Street, seeing this commercial quiet, would smack their heads in frustration, and their black hats would fall on the sidewalk, and one of the little men and women would pick it up and return it, hoping for a verbal thank you, but not expecting the Jew to buy anything as a reward. And the 47th Street Jew, beside himself, would smack his head again, and the whole thing would repeat.

"Is this cute, or what, Josh?"

"It's okay."

"Okay? This is great."

I wondered what the teenagers did for fun. The street wasn't very long, so they couldn't do the country version of my mid-town tour, a big and buzzing loop. And even if this road ran all the way back to New York, it would never get me to kicking my heels, because antique shops and little awnings are margarine, basically margarine.

We walked into a pink candy store just as a fat family was leaving. It looked like my father's old place, with jars of sweets and scoops ready to be held. Difference was this place wasn't right next to a better place. And here, instead of an unsweet David Lipkin behind the counter, was a young guy, couldn't have been more than 20, who took a shine to Manny. He must have seen me, figured me to be 16, and thought that this kid, no way, couldn't be with this hip, hip lady. Baby-sitter. Older sister.

Okay, so he was handsome, nice, had a deep voice and smooth, curly girl-hair. But Manny didn't need to take so long picking which candy she wanted a quarter pound of. And he didn't need to give her eight free taste-samples. And, God knows, they didn't need to giggle just because some candy designer guessed there were enough sweet-tooth writers to buy typewriter-shaped chocolates, or because some folks, honest, just want to buy the black jelly beans.

Manny bought a half-pound mixture.

I asked the Candy Boy if he sold Snickers. He told me to try next door, at the newspaper store.

"You liked him, huh?" We were back on the street.

"Yeah, he was a nice guy."

"You two really hit it off. I mean, you giggled for like ten minutes."

"It's a nice release every now and then, Josh."

I didn't go on. I could tell by the way she used my name that she was getting to anger. I was there already. It was the only time I was ever pissed at her, and I remember it so clearly. Isn't that natural? People remember Pearl Harbor. The only time we ever got hit. A once-in-a-lifetime thing.

Francis didn't answer the door when we rang the bell, so I walked behind a hedge and looked in the window, at him sitting in front of his TV, hitting the air with one hand and sipping from a whisky glass with the other. I rapped on the glass and he turned around. We met at the door.

"Jesus, I'm sorry. I didn't hear you. Did you ring the bell, Manny?"

"Yeah. It's okay."

"Maybe it's busted. No, it's fine. Listen. Hell, you know what it was? I bet I heard the bell and thought it was coming from the TV, 'cause it does kind of sound like the bells on the tube. It's one of those phrase-guessing games. No, I'm not very good at it. I can't think that fast. But they also make it hard on you 'cause they've run out of the popular phrases, so they got these phrases that ain't even phrases. You know what the last one was? Ninety-nine cents. I'm serious. Ninety-nine cents. I mean, what kind of phrase is that? I know people say it, but that don't make it a phrase. People say cheese ball, too, but cheese ball ain't a phrase. If at first you don't succeed, try, try again. There's a phrase. Look at me, standing here while you're there with your bags.

Come on in. Nice lookin' dog. Gert's somewhere around."

Although the sun was out and the house seemed in the right angle to receive it, the inside was dark. The orange rug didn't lighten the place, nor did Francis's hilarious outfit — green jacket, yellow pants, blue shirt. What was it with cops and clothing? Rizzi and Francis. Must be that when they no longer have to wear the dark blue uniform they can go crazy, like an alcoholic who's trapped in a dry town and finally scrapes together enough money for a bus ticket to a liquor store, and a binge. The darkness here came from the walls — the brown, wood paneling that wouldn't let sunlight spread out. Francis had turned on most of his lamps. It was like the Oak Bar at the Plaza, but I got the feeling there was more boozing going on here.

He'd tried to clean up, but he was probably interrupted by the start of his television show. Or maybe he'd had so much to drink that he forgot about the little piles of dust and dog hair that were every few feet on the carpet.

"Sorry about the mess, kids. My vacuum broke last week and I haven't gotten it fixed, so I tried to sweep the carpet, and that's just a pain in the ass."

There was a large photograph of his wife over the fireplace, taken when she was young, in her twenties. A narrow, turned-up nose and soft eyes. Everything about her was soft. The women never seemed to have acne back then. Some of the men did. Mother Mann's boyfriend did. Barkface. Movie man. Another picture caught Manny's eye. Francis with the Henry family, standing on the pond land, the exact spot where Patrick intended to build his house.

"That one's probably about 10 years old, Manny. Will ya look at all the hair on my head. It was like I woke up one morning and all the hair was on the floor by my bed."

"Who are all the people?"

He pointed out Greg and Dorothy. Veronica, Melanie, Patrick, of course, Ellen, Stephanie. Let's see, four young women, and Greg had said there were three daughters. Manny focused on the one most physically different. Tall and thin Ellen, with short, straight black hair. Like Manny, minus the bleaching job.

"Who's Ellen?"

"Sweet girl, Ellen, Patrick's friend at the time. Whenever I look at this picture I can't get over how much hair I had. You know, I haven't had to use a comb in about eight years."

"What ever happened to her?"

"Who, Ellen? Oh, people go their separate ways, you know."

"Were they together long?"

"For some time, yes. You kids hungry? No? Drink? Well, I think I need a refreshment. They say it's good for the heart."

Also on the walls were framed front-page stories in old Boston newspapers. Headlines like "Police Nab Righty In Warehouse" and "Joey the Mouth Gets Life." I quickly scanned the stories looking for Francis's name, but he wasn't there, just the other cops, the guys who spoke for the department and the guys who were particularly heroic that day. The pictures showed the criminals being led away by the cops. Righty, a cocky guy, smiled. He probably had friends everywhere, both sides of the law, wasn't about to let some screwball cops foul up the whole operation. Joey wasn't so cheery. Got life, in the bad sense of the phrase. When you're in the Big House, friends have a funny way of turning their backs to you.

I asked Francis what he had to do with these stories.

"I was there."

"So why aren't you mentioned?"

"They don't want to give grunts like me no credit. Those were the days, though. The bad guys were big, and you didn't care about the little guys. Nowadays, with drugs all over the place, the bad guys are everywhere, and they're little punks, standing on every corner, poisoning the kids. Know what I mean, Josh, drugs everywhere?"

"Yeah." Francis was fishing again.

"And the real big guys live in South America. Can't touch 'em. But there are little punks all over the place, right?"

Next to the newspapers were framed mug shots, profiles and front photos of Righty and Joey. Righty's face seemed discolored on one side. Those were the days, Francis said, when the bad guys had personalities, seemed like they were acting in a play. Righty wasn't no different. Only grew hair on the right side of his face. Well, not exactly only. But the hair on his right grew about twice as fast, so in the afternoon, by the time the left side had a regular shadow, the right side had what looked like a full head of hair. Righty could have been named Lefty. Francis didn't remember how it started. But it's not like Righty was proud of this. Some bad guys liked their names. Three-Piece Warren only wore three-piece suits. The name made sense. And the clothes made him feel classy. But Righty knew the ladies shied away from him because of the hair problem, and he liked the ladies. So he carried a razor with him, or made one of his stooges carry one, and every afternoon, when his face started looking lopsided, he'd order a shave. Didn't matter where he was. In a restaurant, at a ball game, playing poker. He didn't care what he looked like getting a shave, just cared that afterward his face didn't look crooked with hair. The police, for obvious reasons, had taken his razor away several hours before the mug shots were taken, and nature was doing its hairy job on him.

Francis patted Squeaky a little too hard because, more than a drip, she let loose a stream, more volume of urine than I'd seen come out of her at any one time.

"Squeaky!"

"That's okay, Manny. Got a little pissing problem, huh? I get that every now and then, too."

"Where are your paper towels?"

"Just let it be. This carpet takes it all. Guy at the store said I could shit on it and it wouldn't stain."

"I'll just mop it up. The paper towels?"

"If you want, Manny. In the kitchen."

While Manny was gone, Francis asked if it was bad that he was using foul language. I said it was fine. He said it was a hard habit to break. Like smoking, I said. Harder, he said. Manny came back followed by Gert, a German shepherd that seemed the same age as Squeaky, dead in human years. She smelled each of us, and we patted her. Then she approached Squeaky, and the two hit it off immediately. After smelling each other's eyes and ears, Gert slowly collapsed onto her back, into Squeaky's urine, and stuck her legs up. Squeaky, her tail wagging, started licking Gert's toes. But she wasn't peeing anymore. Maybe that's what she had been trying to say to us all along. I love your attention, thank you for it, but you're humans, and the only way I'm going to stop peeing is if I get me some dog.

I said Gert was now going to smell of Squeaky's urine. She's smelled of worse, Francis said. Thirteen years old. Been around.

"You ever had a dog roll in seagull shit? No? That stuff's

152

bad. You got seagulls in New York? I've never been. You believe that? I've lived this long and not gone to New York City."

I could tell that he missed the old days. He looked over at Righty and sighed. He was thinking. Who'd have thought I'd be here, on Cape Cod, in a dark little house with lamps turned on, all these years later, looking at pictures of bad dead guys on my wall, guys that at the time got my cop-blood boiling, and today make me sad 'cause I don't got that fever no more? I should have died in a shoot-out, as long as I took one of them with me. That would have made the papers. Maybe even front page. But would someone have kept a copy? Yeah, the Henrys. Now, getting back to the Henrys.

Francis sat down at the dining room table and we joined him. Next to his glass of whisky was mine, which I'd accepted because the guy had a pull on me. All through my life, my first 16 years, I'd had very few magnets. Jane, maybe Billy. Now, in the course of one week, I'd met two people who pulled me, big-time. Next to my glass was Manny's cup of tea. Francis had also given her some crackers. They were meant to hold cheese, but she dipped them.

"Okay, listen to me, kids. I want to talk about Patrick."

He wanted to get some basic information on paper. He found it helpful to start an investigation with a legal pad. Go slow at first, with a pen, and then take things from there. Nothing begins with a car chase, like it is on TV. But, if you're lucky in this business, you get some action. He asked Manny where she lived, her phone number, in case he wanted to reach her. Where does she work? She thought she might have a business card, pulled out her bridge book, which was on top of everything in her purse. Leanne used to play bridge. Francis never understood it, liked poker instead. You can play poker drunk. Bridge is something different altogether. You got to be smart to play bridge.

"You're a smart one, ain't ya, Manny?"

"Not really. I still don't understand the game. So, I guess I'm not that smart."

"I bet you are, Manny, real smart."

It was just like in the Oak Bar. When Manny went for one item in her wallet she got another, the lock of hair, blond hair. Without looking up, she put it back in its compartment. But I looked up immediately, for Francis, and I found him, and he squinted with suspicion and wrote something down on his legal pad, which, he made sure, we couldn't read. No, she didn't have a business card with her.

"That's okay. What's the name of the place?"

"CPC."

"CBC?"

"No, CPC."

"I got it. What does it stand for?"

"Collins, Prinn, and Corcoran."

"Okay. Collins, Prenn, and Corking. Phone?" She didn't correct him, probably thought he wouldn't come up with anything. I didn't think Manny cared for Francis all that much. He was pushing her. Like I said, he pulled me. Manny gave him the phone number, which he got right on the third go. It didn't bother me that he screwed things up the first time around, that he'd dropped a peanut butter cracker on the motel floor. Manny, though, was impatient to get to the bottom of things and probably saw Francis as another knot in the wood, hard to work around, capable of screwing up what she had to do.

She said she was going to go out for a while, and Francis

got so excited that he downed the last inch of whisky. But Manny didn't ask me to go with her, she needed some time alone, and I didn't offer to go somewhere else, so Francis, seeing that he and I were going to be alone, filled his glass and mine. Manny was going to take a drive around. Francis told her to take her time. The boys would be fine. Boys can always find something to talk about.

"She's pretty, eh Josh?"

"She is."

"You want another drink?"

"Okay."

"Atta boy. So, you got a girlfriend Josh?"

This is what was going on in Francis's head. Like Dorothy, he thought I was sleeping with Manny, that I'd been shtupping her Mondays, Wednesdays, and Fridays while Patrick got his share Tuesdays, Thursdays, and Saturdays, leaving Sunday as the day of rest, because Manny, like the Big Boy, needed some shut-eye. Maybe I'd been content with the schedule for a while, because she was a find, and a piece of something is better than no piece at all, but I was young, active, and three days just weren't enough. As a psycho, I didn't think things out soberly. I bumped him off. Maybe Manny played a part. Couldn't bring herself to tell Patrick to get lost. She had a thing for young guys, and I was young, and her passion got the better of her, gave me the go-ahead. I stood behind her door on a Tuesday, his day, and when Patrick opened the door, humming a happy tune because he was going to get some action, I hit him on the head, ending the humming, ending the life. The body? There are a million places to get rid of a dead body, particularly in a place like New York. There are rivers. And dumpsters on every corner. The guys who drive the garbage trucks don't get paid enough to distinguish the sound of a crushed chicken bone from a crushed human bone, crushed produce from crushed Patrick.

Just in case Francis needed to reach me, could I give him my home phone. I gave him Billy's. Work? I gave him the right number. I thought his suspicion of me would wear off, that even if he was a bad dick he'd realize I wasn't worth going after. He'd never call. That would be an interesting conversation. "Mr. Lipkin, my name is Francis." "So fucking what?" But it wouldn't happen.

"Your eyes are all red, Josh. Everything okay?"

"Yeah. It's just the whisky, I think. I'm not used to drinking in the middle of the day."

"Can I ask you a question?"

"Sure."

"You won't be insulted?"

"No."

"Do you do drugs? I know a lot of youngsters do it these days."

Patrick's murder had nothing to do with my need to have Manny sex seven days a week. No, it was a drug thing. Manny was one of my dealers. Sure, I was young, but I was a good businessman, had women like Manny all over the city. Always women. Patrick bought some stuff from me, on credit. I let some people do that. But he didn't feel like paying, did he, and I wasn't about to let word get out that I was soft. I had no choice. Could have broken his legs, I guess. But they don't do that anymore. You got to whack 'em, send a lesson to your other customers that they'll lose more than their legs if they get all goofy on you. I mean, legs don't carry the same weight that they used to. Or I sold Patrick some bad stuff, and he wandered into a corner of the city, maybe near Grant's Tomb, intending to get high, and he succeeded more than he'd hoped. So high he wouldn't come down.

"No. I mean, I'll smoke some pot, but not a lot. Did Patrick do drugs?"

"Did?"

"What?"

"You said did."

"Oh. Does Patrick?"

The past tense problem, again. I think Francis wrote "did" on his legal pad.

"And you're Jewish, aren't you?"

"What does that have to do with anything?"

"Nothing. Hey, I'm Catholic. No big deal. In my book, there's plenty of room for all faiths. Hell, I haven't been to church in years, not since Leanne died, God Bless Her."

I was a rich Jew and had hired a hit man to take care of Patrick because 1) I wanted an exclusive on Manny sex, 2) Patrick had somehow angered me, the head of a Jewish drug ring, 3) Patrick had borrowed some money from me, a rich Jew, and, hey, business is business, 4) Patrick had been doing some clandestine work for that group, the PLO, and if he had it in for Israel, I had no choice but to have it in for him, because you got to believe in something.

I answered all of Francis's questions. I thought I would enjoy playing with him more, but I wanted it to end. Sometimes, when you're riding a roller-coaster, as fun as it is, you want to get off. Maybe you'll go on again. Maybe you'll just go home and go to sleep. Or you'll walk down the arcade and buy some taffy from the guy whose pulling machine actually works.

"Listen, Francis. I know you want to get to the bottom of this and you think you got to ask me all these questions. But they're a waste of time. I had nothing to do with this. I never met the guy. I'm just helping Manny look for him."

"I'm just asking questions, kid."

So I asked him why he went into our motel room. He thought about denying it, but realized that I wouldn't have brought it up unless I knew. Oh that.

"I was just looking for you guys, before you went over to Dorothy and Greg's."

"Why'd you go inside when we weren't there?"

Again, he said, old habit. Yeah. Crosby had let him in. Did he find anything? He wasn't looking for anything. Sorry. We'd found a peanut butter cracker. So that's how we knew. Yeah. It was on the floor. I love those peanut butter crackers, Josh. And Doc likes 'em.

"Josh, did you see the hair Manny was carrying?" Yes, the blond hair in the wallet.

"No."

"She had a lock of blond hair in her wallet."

"So?"

"Well, she ain't a blond. That bleaching job doesn't make her a blond."

"What are you getting at?"

"And she doesn't have any kids."

"I know."

"So whose hair is it?"

"I don't know."

"It's the same color as Patrick's. That's all I'm saying."

I'd never doubted her. Not really. Only a crazy could

have fooled me, and Manny didn't seem the Bellevue type.

"Listen, Josh. You seem like a nice kid. But you're young, you got life ahead of you. I got a lot behind me, maybe too much. But I've seen a lot of things. And I've learned a little bit."

He wanted to tell me a couple of stories, about the past, his past, about some disappearances. One was a woman. The other, a man. Crime was the bottom line. Yeah, I'll have another.

Guy's name was Osborne, a butler for this rich dame on Beacon Hill. But I'm getting ahead of myself, as Leanne used to say. Get it? Get it? In bed? Leanne said this a lot, Josh, and it took me a while to get it.

So this case comes in to Sean, best damn detective I ever saw, and, boy, did he dress nice. Just like three-piece Warren. This heiress had disappeared, vanished into thin air, and immediately Sean smells something rotten, 'cause he was good, had a nose. I'm told to help him out. I wanted to be a detective and the Captain had a soft spot for me, before he died, of course, and said I couldn't get any better experience than to tag along with Sean. The lady lived in this mansion, had some kind of foundation in her name. Old money. Only guy who had any regular contact with her was Osborne, the butler. But he didn't have a motive, as far as we knew. Got along great with the lady, was in her will, but only for some small change. He'd have a better life as long as she was breathing, see. There was no body. Osborne just called the precinct one day, saying the woman hadn't returned from some function, and he was worried. Sean and me go over to the place, a palace really, and we talk to him, a nice enough guy, in his sixties, quiet. I mean, we know the butler did it, like the line goes, right, but we don't got a body, don't got any idea why. Osborne had a plum life, was a servant, sure, but from what we'd been told, the old lady treated him fine.

Sean gets drunk one night, off duty, and walks in front of a train. Smack. Dead. Blood all over his nice suit. Limbs all over the place. It's gonna take a week to get another detective on the case. We're all blocked up. I see this as my opportunity, you know, to make a name for myself. So I sneak into the house one afternoon and see Osborne making up some tea and putting some little cookies on a plate, and I think, well, he's just making himself a snack. But it wasn't for him. He walks the stuff into the library, puts it on a table in front of the fireplace, and says "your tea ma'am, will there be anything else?" Guy lost all his marbles. Later, I get a call from the lady's lawyer, says she was going to sell the house and move out west, to Arizona or something. He just thought I should know. All right, so I got a motive, see, the butler was going to lose his job, maybe the old lady wasn't going to offer him something out there. But I still don't got any evidence, physical I mean. I sneak in again, and the guy does the same tea and cookie thing. The fire's going, only this time he says something different. "Is the fire too hot, ma'am?" and he walks over to the fire place and starts poking around. And whenever he pokes he says "Excuse me. Excuse me." Like he's poking her. We hadn't checked the fireplace, Sean and Me, when we looked over the house.

I come back the next day with Mahoney, the detective who took over for Sean, and we ask Osborne if we can look around some more. We walk straight to the fireplace, and Osborne must know it's over, 'cause he says "the madam is hot." She certainly was. He'd burned up most of her, but some of her bones were in the back of the fireplace, charred but still together. The lady had gone up in smoke. I asked him right there, point blank, if he'd killed her, and I'll never forget what he said. "It's very dry in Arizona." Honest to God.

"So what happened?"

The case was all over the papers. It was one of those sensational stories. Mahoney took all the credit. Figures. The guy on top wants nothing else but to stay there. The Captain knew it was me who'd done the work, but he died a couple of months after all of this, and the new guy was an old buddy of Mahoney's and stuck by him.

"What about Osborne?"

Killed himself. Second day in jail. Got his hands on a knife and stabbed himself in the throat. Didn't slice it, stabbed it. Hard to believe anybody could actually do that. Then again, hard to believe anybody would burn his boss up and then serve her tea.

So this lady calls me up one day, not long after I've left the force, when I'm just starting to do some things on the side. Tells me her husband's disappeared, and could I look for him. Woman sounds like she's got dough, so I say, $150 a day, that's what I cost. Whatever it takes, she says, just please find Arnold. So I bite. The money was good, and I was itching, 'cause I'd been out of the action for a while, and it's tough that way. So I meet with her, and you know the things you hear, movies and stuff, about these gorgeous blonds with veils on their heads and legs up to here walking into your office and crying about poor, disappeared Arnold?

Well, it might be true in the movies, but this lady is ugly, big square jaw, big square head, almost like a guy dressed up as a woman, know what I mean?

"Yeah. I've been there."

"Huh?"

"Nothing."

Arnold owned two stores, sold appliances, didn't show up for work on a Monday, didn't show up at home that night. Just didn't show up anywhere. The police were investigating, but they were slow, and I should know, right? She wanted someone to devote full time to this, what did she call it?, tragedy. So I check everything out, to see if he's skipped off on his wife or something, check bank accounts and stuff, but he hasn't drawn any money, and you don't skip without cash. I have no idea where the guy is, and she says they got along great, but I get wind that they used to take separate vacations, which I guess might not tell you all that much, but he had a thing for prostitutes, and when he went his way, he sampled the local cuisine, you know what I'm saying? And I bring this up to the woman, and she knows all about it, I can tell, but doesn't like the fact that I know, for some reason. Then she says maybe a hooker killed him, 'cause they don't got any morals. But hookers rarely kill, and when they do, you find the body pretty fast. I could have asked her about her husband's morals, but I didn't. Did she stand to inherit all his money? Yes, but please don't think I'm involved, because why would I have asked you to help me? She asked me if I was married. Happily, I said. She said that was nice.

So this is what happens. Arnold doesn't turn up anywhere. The police close the case. They think she did it, but they don't have nothing. She pays me, says she's glad we tried. No one can say she didn't try. And guess what? I take Leanne out to dinner a few weeks later and we bump into her. She's all dressed up, not that it did her face any good, and she's with this guy. She introduces him, named Stuart, seemed kind of shady, and I introduce Leanne. We chat, and I say we're going to take a boat ride in the harbor, and I guess I'd had a fair amount to drink because Leanne tells me later that I asked that woman something like three times whether she enjoyed boats. I don't know why I said it. Couldn't remember any of it. But Leanne says the woman got all flushed and walked away, with Stuart doing his best to keep up.

A week later, I'm sitting in my office, downtown, when I get this knock on my door. Come in. This woman I'd never seen before, dressed in this tight short skirt, sits down and in this breathy voice gives me this story, all confused, about someone trying to blackmail her or something, I couldn't get it straight, and anyway she seemed more interested in talking about my payment than about the problem. She said she didn't have any money, but she could pay in another way, get it, and she stands up and walks over to me. Now, she's ugly, see, real ugly. The tight dress didn't make up for that. And besides, I never cheated on Leanne. Never. So she moves to sit on my lap and before she does I stand up and say no thanks. And she runs out of my office. Strange, I thought. What's worse, same thing happens the following week, only with a different woman, gives me a line about her dog being lost and offers to pay me in the, uh, unconventional sense. But she's ugly, too, and I never cheated on Leanne. Again, I stand up, no thanks, and, again, she runs out.

"I don't get it."

The first lady, the wife, the one who killed Arnold, must have killed him on a boat, or near a boat, well there must have been a boat there somewhere, and when we met at the restaurant, she thought I was trying to tell her that I knew all about it, I had the skinny. Course I didn't, but she didn't know that. So she hired these bimbos to, you know what, hoping that I'd do it and then she could keep me silent. She was trying to even the score, get a two-way blackmail going. I didn't fall for it though. I still didn't have any evidence, nothing I could have gone to the cops with. I just went on with my life. You know, I liked the fact that there was this killer out there, probably biting her nails every day, wondering if I was going to turn her in.

"Were you worried?"

"Nah. She wouldn't dare come after me. I never heard from her again, and nothing about her. She could have died, or be living somewhere still, biting her nails, thinking I got it on her."

"Amazing."

"Ain't it? Let me tell you something, Josh. I don't believe in accidents. I think everything's got an explanation. You just got to dig for it."

"Yeah, but the answer isn't always what you think it is."

"True. I been wrong and I been right. Only God's keeping the score."

"You believe in God, Francis?"

"Not really. Scratch that score business. What kind of God do Jews believe in?"

"No idea. I spend more time in St. Patrick's than in temple."

I was lying on the bed, getting ready for a whisky nap. I'd never taken one before 'cause I'd never been alcohol-dizzy in the middle of the day. The door was closed, and I could hear Francis talking, but I didn't try to listen in. I was thinking about what he'd said before. The stories. Sure, those capers were way out there. And Francis might have exaggerated them. If the past wasn't that interesting, if it really was as boring as the present, then he'd have nothing to live for.

For a few minutes, as I stared at Francis's tacky lighthouse lamp across the room, the stories affected me as Francis had wanted them to. Maybe Manny had done it. Why did Manny keep blond hair in her wallet? Was this the hair that she'd cut from Patrick's head after she'd hit him over the head with one of her cast-iron bench planes? She'd talked in her sleep the night before, mentioned a plane, cursed at Patrick. They'd had a fight and, bang, down it came. It had been one of her father's tools. The more I knew, the more I seemed to know, the more I doubted.

But Francis had said the bottom line was always crime. That was his Dick Tracy world. I'd disappeared, too, and it had nothing to do with crime. Just a need, more powerful than any itch, to get away. Francis was the type who saw what he wanted to see, and to hell with reality. Good guys and bad guys. Black hats and white hats. There are no accidents.

I had a bad sleep. Kept sweating and needed to drink some water every five minutes. I wondered if this was my mother's sleeping habit. When you're driven to this type of thing on a daily basis, you got to be driving pretty hard away from something. Daddy. Always the answer. And Francis, too. Driven from the present. Booze is tough. Makes you sentimental, nostalgic for a better time, but whacks you with hopelessness, tells you that you can't go back and that the future looks as bad as what you got now.

I was awake when Manny returned. My anxiety was like this. Twenty percent booze (because that's what it does to you), thirty percent fearing that Manny was a murderer and a loon who'd strung me along, forty percent cursing myself for being a gullible son of a bitch who, if Francis had told me the moon was made of blue cheese, would have been grateful the moon is so far away because I hate blue cheese. That left ten percent for the nitty-gritty tensions. My family. My future. Whether I was ever going to lose my virginity, or, if I had, whether history would repeat itself.

I was slow with whisky when Manny got back. She was wearing a tight black sweater. Amazing that she wasn't sweating. Thin sweater. It complemented her breasts. Again, I thought about sex, and how I wanted it for the first or second time, this time with Manny. But I needed to talk to her first. She said she needed to speak to Francis. He came out of the kitchen. But I said I needed to talk to her first. "Please." I told her to come outside with me, walk down the street. Francis asked if everything was okay. I nudged Manny out the door.

Francis followed us, and did a piss-poor job of it, in the sense that he let on what he was doing as soon as he started doing it. I heard the front door slam after him. He stood by the mailbox, froze, but then realized that I saw him and opened the box up, like he was looking for mail. He was looking for mail the entire time Manny and I talked. We walked halfway down the street.

"What's wrong, Josh?"

It started out like the conversation we'd had in the Park, when she laid the Manny as Man joke on me. I jumbled my words, fell over 'em, told her I didn't want this to sound weird and hoped she wouldn't take this the wrong way. She said she needed to get back and talk to Francis.

"That lock of hair you keep in your wallet."

"Yeah?"

"Whose hair is it?"

"Why?" I said Francis had brought it up. Patrick's hair.

"What?"

"Well, you know he's suspicious. He's suspicious of me, too. And he's looking for things that confirm it, that's all. But he just said the hair in your wallet was the same color as Patrick's hair."

"Jesus Christ, Josh, what are you saying?"

"I don't know."

"What if it was his hair? Would that be weird?"

"Yeah. I guess. I mean, I think so."

"Well it's not. Shit. I wouldn't keep his hair in my wallet."

"It's not his? Then whose?"

"It's mine."

"You don't have blond hair."

"I did when I was real young, until I was like five. Then it darkened."

"But why do you have it?"

"It might sound a little sentimental, but my father used to keep it in his wallet. I should take it out, but I haven't for some reason. I keep the bridge book in my purse, too, and it doesn't need to be there, with the amount that I've learned. I just carry both my parents around with me in some way."

"So you were a blond." I smiled big-time.

"What would you have thought if it was Patrick's hair?"

"Um..."

"That I'd killed him, and kept the hair like a memento of my crime?"

"Manny, I'm sorry. I don't know what's going on in my head."

When she was crying on the library steps, I'd put my hand on her shoulder. When we were sitting in the park, when she was pretending to be Manny Man, she'd put her hand on my knee. And, when she was talking in her sleep, when the nightmares hit, I'd pressed up against her. But now we had our first, real face-to-face contact, and it was she, taking my shoulders, who pulled me close.

"Listen, Josh. You've helped me keep my sanity, right?"

"I have?"

"Yeah. And I'm going to help you keep yours."

"Okay."

"Don't let old Francis put ideas into your head. I wouldn't be surprised if he and the Crosbys were related."

"Francis isn't all that bad."

"What the fuck is he thinking? I'm carrying Patrick's hair in my wallet?"

"The Henrys are like family to him. That's all."

"Well, Patrick was getting to be like family to me."

That was some serious statement. I could have been jealous, I guess, but I was still glad that she'd been a blond, when she was a little girl called Tiffany. She said she needed to get back to Francis. We turned and saw him scurrying back to the house, trying his darndest to blend in with the shrubbery, but the shrubbery was green and stationary, and he was a big, moving, white man. When we walked inside,

Francis was quenching his thirst whisky-style, panting, watching a game show, and pretending he'd never left his seat, that he was panting because, you know, those game shows can really lather you up.

Manny had driven down to the docks, checked out those big working boats named after wives and girlfriends, talked to some guys who work on the water and come home smelling of salt and fish. They knew Gregory. An honest guy, wasn't born a fisherman but was good at it, and would gladly throw work to some of the boys, harbor rats, who were having a tough time making ends meet. And he even helped them figure out their insurance, which could be a bear because it's not like you're working for a big corporation that hires folk to push papers on your behalf. They asked her how she knew Greg, and she brought up Patrick, her boyfriend. One of the harbor rats called below deck for Stevie, and he climbed out of the boat carrying a wooden box full of ice cubes and fish parts. Stevie had huge muscles, had carried a lot of those boxes, but he had a baby face, gentle. Said he had nothing against Greg. Hell, Greg had thrown him some work last fall. But Patrick — sorry, lady. Don't got nothing kind to say about Patrick.

They talked while he was standing on the boat and she was standing on the blacktop, where trucks pull up to haul the day's catch away. Stevie and Patrick had been good friends once, in high school, listened to the same music, knew each other's locker combinations, wrestled on the school team together, went light on each other because they didn't want to see any injuries. They'd go to Stevie's house after school to cook up some macaroni and cheese. Dorothy hadn't liked Patrick going off so often, but that's how teenagers are. She would call Stevie's house when Patrick was over, and the boys would just let the phone ring. The phone would ring steadily for an hour. On weekend nights, Patrick and Stevie would take some beer from Stevie's fridge and walk down to the beach, and Stevie, who knew something about stars, would outline the constellations with his index finger and talk about the difference between comets and meteors. Patrick knew art, would go on about Rembrandt, particularly liked that Jewish Bride picture. Those were some great nights.

Problem started when Stevie started going out with this girl, the girl who would become his wife, but only after Patrick stole her. Stevie didn't know why he did it, maybe because Patrick couldn't understand that Stevie now wanted to spend his weekend nights with Ellen. Yeah, the same Ellen, from the picture. But Patrick was better looking than Stevie, and Ellen fell for Patrick Boy, even though she knew it was the wrong thing to do. Patrick Boy screwed her up, fucked with her head, and that was even before he disappeared, which really messed her up. Yeah, the disappearing act was just the icing on the fucking cake. It took Ellen a whole year to get over the disappeared asshole. Stevie ended up marrying her. Got two great kids.

Stevie wouldn't elaborate on Patrick. After all these years, he still got upset thinking about it. Patrick was the only person he had ever really wanted to hurt. Funny, in a sad way, because they had once gone light on each other in wrestling practice. Said he felt bad for Manny, really knew what she was going through. Said it's better to be alone than to be with an asshole. Said he didn't want to sound insensitive, but he hoped she didn't find Patrick.

"Why didn't you or anyone else mention this, Francis? I mean, Christ, I'm busting my ass trying to find Patrick and

I hear something like this."

"Easy does it, Manny." Francis turned off the TV.

"Easy does it? Greg started to tell us this last night, right? But Dorothy stopped him. She said this had all happened when he was a kid. Made it sound like he was just a little boy who ran away because his parents wouldn't buy him a goddamned skateboard or something."

"It was a long time ago."

"But he wasn't a kid. He was like 18 years old. And it sounds like he broke this woman's heart. Ellen's. He totally screwed her up."

"Well, relationships sometimes don't work out."

"Is this for real? Are you for real?"

"Listen Manny, it's true that Patrick ran away. He was just scared about getting too involved with Ellen. You've been scared before, haven't you?"

I thought about Manny walking the streets of New York, avoiding her hospitalized father because the sight of him was too much for her.

"Of course I have, but this is different, and you know it, don't you? Don't you? We're going to leave first thing in the morning, if that's okay with you."

These were the biggest mood swings of the week. I'd not seen Manny so angry, and Francis, newer to my life, seemed for the first time really unsure about something. The confidence was off him, a man naked to the world, a naked man who was embarrassed by his body and was desperately grabbing for clothing that was beyond his reach.

I would have helped Manny with anything, and maybe that meant joining her against Francis, but I felt bad for him. There's nothing worse than an old person who's sad. I'd seen enough of them in my nursing home career. And

Francis was like that, head down. He was turning the newspaper pages faster than he could ever read them, occasionally looking over the top to see if someone's mood had changed. He didn't drink.

That night Manny took care of her anger by working on her guitar, gluing some Mother of Fucking Pearl shells into the instrument's neck. She did this in her room, while she listened to some of her rapid-fire music. Francis cheered himself up by making a big salami sandwich, which he split with me. We played gin. I had a hangover, at a time when most people think about starting to drink. Over the dining room table, where we were playing cards, I told Francis what I'd wanted to tell him before, but didn't because he and Manny had gone at it. I said that Manny had been a blond. He didn't say anything, just picked from the pile and discarded a three of clubs. I said it again. "A blond." "I heard ya the first time." The present was once again disappointing him. He threw another three.

It was the middle of the night and I couldn't sleep. I put on my jeans and walked into Manny's room. I sat next to her, put my hand on her shoulder, asked her if she was awake, and she woke up. The moon was on her face. The sun wasn't allowed to enter the house, but the moon was given the red carpet. I asked her if she was okay. I was sorry that she had to hear what that guy Stevie had to say. She yawned.

"You know, I feel I've learned more about Patrick in the few days I've been away from him than in the ten months I've spent with him."

I squeezed her shoulder. I was ready to get into bed with her. She fell asleep. I heard a noise and turned toward the door, saw Francis standing there. His face was dark, so I couldn't see what expression he had on.

Francis had called my father. That's who he had been talking to when I was sinking into my whisky-nap. But I'm getting ahead of myself, as Leanne used to say to Francis. Get it? Get it? In bed? We got up and had some breakfast. Dorothy stopped by to say she was sorry to see us go. Manny was polite, and for her sake I didn't say anything. Of course, I imagined messing up Dorothy's cement hair, wrestling her to the ground, calling Squeaky over, positioning the dog's rear over Dorothy's face, and petting Squeaky like there was no tomorrow, so she'd better let all her urine out now. We loaded the car, put Squeaky in the back. Dorothy took both of Manny's hands. Stay in touch, Manny. No mention of Patrick.

Then it happened, and the next few minutes happened fast. A silver Mercedes screeched into the driveway, and I could see my father's angry face through the windshield. It was Genius Uncle Saul's car. I stepped closer to our VW. Manny asked who the guy was.

"Shit. It's my father."

I told Manny to get in the car. She didn't understand. I told her again. "Get in the car."

Francis walked up to the Mercedes. Maybe he was going to greet my father. Maybe he expected a parent who was concerned that his little baby boy had lost his way and craved the warmth of Daddy. What he got was a red-faced David Lipkin who kept his hands wrapped up in fists and used one of them to push Francis out his way and used the other to smash my cheekbone. I saw it coming, but his punch was faster than my head, and the connection hurt like hell.

Dorothy put her hand to her mouth. Manny yelled. I told her to start the car. David Lipkin grabbed my shirt.

"What the hell do you think you're doing, pulling this shit on your mother? You want to embarrass me, that what you want? Jesus Fucking Christ, I have to borrow my brother's fucking car. What do I look like, a fucking idiot?"

"Fuck you." I pushed him away, with just enough time to get into the Rabbit and lock the door. He pounded on the window, screamed "fuck" a few times. I told Manny to go, and she stalled. Did this a couple of times. Francis approached my father, told him to calm down, but David Lipkin tried to punch him. Although he was getting up there, Francis had been around, on the streets, I mean, and he blocked my father's punch, and threw his own into David Lipkin's stomach, which hurt David Lipkin, because his mouth opened wide, his eyes turned up into his brain, and he fell onto the ground. Manny finally got the car into first and we hurled forward, smack into the Mercedes, denting it. The Rabbit was fine. My father screamed. Manny turned us around and we moved down the street. Part of me wanted to sink into the seat, to see nothing, but a bigger part — and I think this part would win out in most folks — kept me looking out the rear window. I saw my father get up. I saw Francis telling Dorothy something. I saw Francis get in his car. My father did the same. But he got out and looked around the ground. Must have dropped his keys, poor guy.

Francis followed us down the street, onto the highway, back to New York. His black Chevy was never far behind us. He was trying to hide, make it so we couldn't see him. He slid behind a car that was behind us, but when that car exited to the right, he didn't find another to block our view. So he slowed down, finally. Gave us the room he should have given us in the first place.

Manny asked if I was okay, if I needed a doctor. I wouldn't let myself cry in front of her, but, boy, did I ever want to. All the junk in my life was floating to the surface. And my cheek hurt something awful.

She asked me about my father. I told her I was sorry that I hadn't gotten the chance to introduce her.

6

So I told Manny about my father, how he slapped me around and cleaned the apartment with a vacuum and a toothbrush, how he loved me about as much as he loved smudged glass, how he was the worst businessman in the history of New York City, despite being a Jew, and that David Lipkin got to be David Lipkin either because of Genius Uncle Saul or a short circuit in the brain. My mother hadn't been sober since the 1970s, since the candy store sank, and she didn't wear the booze well, not like Francis anyway. Yeah, she was like that because David Lipkin was David Lipkin, and because her parents had been too old, should have been thinking about retirement, not shitty diapers. I'd never wanted siblings.

I knew my age lie was up. Manny wondered why my father had come to Cape Cod, why he'd come after me. It was like I was a kid. A child. You don't do that kind of thing if your son is a grownup, even if you're upset, right? I mean, an adult is an adult, and you can do what you want, without committing a crime or anything.

"And your father shows up, screaming about how you've

hurt your mother by running away." It makes as much sense as Barkface, Mother Mann's man, telling us to look for the chiaroscuro in the movie we had no intention of seeing.

I told Manny I wasn't as old as I might have let on. Not eighteen. Not seventeen, either. Sixteen? Yes, sixteen. I was born in 1967.

"Jesus Christ. I was a sophomore in high school in 1967."

"I know."

"I was listening to the Stones when you were listening to lullabies."

"Yeah."

"I'm nearly twice as old as you."

"I know."

"Jesus Christ. Well, you're the most mature sixteen-year-old I've ever met."

At another time, I might have been flattered. I guess I was mature. Dealt with the world like an older guy, handled the shit in my life as though I'd been born in the first half of the 60s, maybe even the late 50s. Other kids I knew played a lot of sports, did a lot of drugs, watched a lot of TV, giggled about sex, when they weren't boasting about it. Sure, I had pimples, thought about having sex for the first or second time, had my childish pleasures, like baiting the Crosbys or playing cat and mouse games with Francis. But I was no kid.

Particularly with Manny. That was the thing. I mean, Manny and I had an even relationship, one to one, something she'd never had with her brother, who wasn't around when she was a kid and who was still a kid when she became an adult. I felt we were a team. I didn't want her to step back, make us look like one of those kid/grownup buddy movies.

Two years might not sound like a lot, from 18 to 16. But tell that to the mother of a three-year-old baby boy who, 24-months before, was learning how to say "mama" and now says "why" to everything, like when you tell him to chew with his mouth closed. Tell that to an old timer who, in the past two years, has gone from healthy to having one lung, scaly skin that itches, a tube pumping vitamin drink up his nose, and eyes with clouds in 'em, which isn't necessarily a bad thing because if he had good eyes he'd be able to make out the white walls of the hospital room and read the chart on the end of the bed, the chart that says it won't be long now. The chart's in doctor-code, of course, but it's been 24 months of hell, and part of that hell is learning how to decipher the fuckin' chart.

And two years means a lot with sex. An 18-year-old is a damn good find, see, but a 16-year-old is a crime, puts you in the Big House, baby, sharing space with folks who'll gladly do a number on your face, or another part of you, because there aren't too many rules Inside, and none of 'em is Love Thy Neighbor. Yeah, I thought about sex and Manny and me and the future, and it didn't look good.

But mostly, I didn't want her to think that I was a kid who couldn't handle her, a kid who was only interested in getting some sweet taffy to make the saliva run and turn the tongue bright purple.

Thank God she hadn't giggled and guessed about the specifics of my running away. I'd left at 3:30 in the afternoon, a sobbing mess, when Mommy said two oatmeal cookies were enough, that I had to save some room for the juicy pork loin roast. I'd left at 6:00 in the evening, when Daddy said a skateboard was out of the question, that delivery trucks and cabs would eat me for breakfast and spit me back on the street.

"So when you saw me that morning in the park, you'd run away?"

"Yeah. I mean, I didn't know then that I wouldn't go back. I realized that later."

"You could have told me all this, Josh."

"You've been going through your own stuff."

"And you've helped me, right? Like I said before, you've helped me keep my sanity. I want to be there for you, too."

"Thanks. I'm okay."

"All this running away."

"What?"

"I was just thinking about people running away."

"You mean Patrick?"

"I don't know. Maybe."

"You think he ran away?"

"Who knows? You know what's weird? All yesterday I was thinking about him, you know, what happened to him, what he might have done. I haven't thought about him at all today, until just now. Not at all."

She shook her head and got quiet. I let her think about not thinking about Patrick. And she let me think about returning to life as a sixteen-year-old, about going back to New York. You can only be a runaway for so long. You either have to go back or set up shop somewhere else.

She dropped me off at Billy's. Asked if this was my home. Yes and no, I told her. We'd hook up later. She had to try to remove Squeaky's pee stain, and if she couldn't, explain to the VW guys that they'd overlooked this stain when they gave her the car, and she had to deal with a gross urine smell the entire way to and back from Cape Cod, and how does that figure in the bogus rental agreement?

I was down and Billy was out. His mother said he was tutoring a Harlem kid in a summer school program, had been doing it for a few weeks. I had no idea. I never thought Billy was selfish. Just thought math was his own world, something that would have lost some of its appeal if he shared it. I once asked him for help with an algebra problem — graphing an equation or something else as useful as a spoon with a hole through the middle — and he went so fast, said it was so obvious, that I got pissed. And I got the problem wrong.

Now, Billy was helping a kid, and it was during summer, when he could have been doing his favorite thing, smoking pot, lying on his bed, drawing pictures of "8" falling on its side. Thirty percent of me — look at me, using numbers. Professor Billy would be happy — was proud of him, but a whopping seventy percent was pissed, not at Billy, but at me, for not having anything to tutor, or even share. I guess I needed my own accomplishments before I could be happy for anybody else's, and I didn't have a one. Maybe I wasn't as mature as Manny had said.

Billy's mom asked me about Cape Cod. She'd heard it was beautiful. God, she hadn't been to a beach in years. God, the idea that some people actually think about tan lines. God, she'd be embarrassed to get into a bathing suit, if she could find one that fit her, because she hadn't put on her old one since she had Billy, and babies stretch things out, you know. She made me a peanut butter and jelly sandwich, and I told her everything, from the Crosbys to Dorothy, from Bill Richmond to Stevie's bad blood with Patrick, from Francis to David Lipkin's borrowed Mercedes. She knew about the David Lipkin part.

"He called yesterday to see if I had a car he could use. He was bullshit about you, which isn't unusual. I tried to tell him that you just needed some space, and he called me a hippie and hung up."

"A hippie?"

"Hey, I've been called worse."

She didn't seem to care about Francis. I'd described his big, boozy body and the butler story and the one about the dame who did in her appliance hubby and sent two square-jawed dames to do a blackmailing number on the dick with the goods. But she was more concerned about me, my screwed-up life.

"What are you going to do, Josh?"

"About what?"

"About your father, your home, your family. You know what I'm talking about."

I walked over to the window and looked down onto First Avenue, at the traffic jam that was the same as when I'd left, at the stores that were the same, the neon lights that hadn't gone out, at the bums who hadn't woken up. Francis was new, leaning against a Mexican restaurant. He must have loved it, being in New York for the first time, and on a case, too. His head was cocked, but the sun was in his eyes, and even with his hand as a visor, he couldn't see me. I hadn't told Billy's mom that the PI had followed us back to the city, and I sure wasn't going to mention that he was checking out her apartment. She didn't know Francis like I did. Would have freaked her out, I think. She was the type, strong, to go out and confront him, maybe poke him in the

181

stomach with an umbrella.

"I don't know what I'm gonna do."

She said, of course, I could stay there, but I needed to think long-term. I either had to work it out with my parents — "I'm not saying that's gonna be easy" — or make a clean break, somehow, and she didn't know what that involved. "I'd be happy to adopt you, if that's what it takes to give you something better." One of the sweetest things I've ever heard anybody say. That would have made Billy, the tutor, my brother. I could have done worse. He'd teach me, and maybe I'd learn something that I could teach him. I could come home every day and not cringe before walking inside. There wouldn't even be a mezuza to ignore.

I went to see my mother, just in case what my father had said about her being upset was true. I still had a soft spot. As much as you want or need to turn your back, it's your mom, the person who in better days might have tickled you in the belly or fed you as many oatmeal cookies as you want because they're good — screw the pork loin roast — and you're her son. Francis seemed to panic when I left Billy's building. As before, in the car and on his street, he showed that he didn't have that detective talent of making himself scarce, not letting on what he's up to. He walked on the opposite side of the street, directly across from me. Sometimes I'd stop, just to see what he would do, and he'd stop also, and three times guys with briefcases bumped into him. One of those out-of-towners who doesn't get the New York walking thing and can't help but screw it up.

The liquor store was on the way, but I would have walked by it if it was in New Jersey, just to make sure my father was there, not at home. His back was to the street window. He was putting the expensive scotch closer to the cash register, so people who didn't know what they wanted or made the mistake of asking for advice, assuming that my father was honest, would be showed the Glenlivet long before the J&B. Raoul saw me, waved, and was about to say something when I put my finger to my lips. He said something to my father and came outside to me, around the corner.

"Hey, Josh, you all right?"

"Yeah, how you doin'?"

"Your papa was pretty pissed at you, man."

"Tell me about it."

"He track you down?"

"Yeah."

"Where were you, somewhere in Carolina?"

"Cape Cod."

"Oh. Where's that?"

"Massachusetts."

"Massachusetts? I got a cousin in Boston."

"I gotta go Raoul. Don't tell my father I been around."

"You got it, Josh."

"See you around." I started to leave.

"Josh."

"Yeah?"

"Your papa left me alone in the store when he went after you. The first time I been alone here."

"Good for you, Raoul."

"I stole a bottle of Glenlivet."

"I won't tell."

"I know you won't. I just needed to tell you. See ya. Hey Josh?"

"Yeah?"

"That Glenlivet's good. Goes down smooth."

I, of course, was a whisky man.

So I touched the mezuza on the way in. I didn't kiss my fingers or anything. No religion involved. Hell, I had to look up mezuza in the dictionary to spell it right, and to make sure I understood what it really is. "...a small piece of parchment inscribed with the Shema, from Deuteronomy (6:4-9 and 11: 13-21), rolled and put into a case and attached to the doorpost of the home, as commanded in the Biblical passages." Wow. I guess I could also look up Shema, but enough is enough.

Okay, so I expected my mother to be different, moved to one side or the other. Either upped her booze count and decided that dressing each day and doing her hair were a waste of time, or stopped cold turkey and taken a job counseling alcoholics on how to turn life around. No, she was the same. Sipping vodka. Letting the fan blow her hair into blinders. Eating dry toast with sugar on it, sugar that the fan blew into the air and onto her lap and the floor. Never changing the TV channel, never changing her expression, even when the program gave way to commercials. One thing my mother, God Bless Her Soul, taught me is to hate television.

"Sweetie, Josh, there you are. I've been so worried. Come here and give your mother a kiss."

She wanted contact. I walked over and kissed her on the cheek, careful not to inhale, because I didn't want to smell her in any way. Grabbed some potato chips and sat down at the table with my mother and the television.

"How are you, Josh?"

"Fine, ma, how are you?"

Her eyes, staring at the screen, could not have gotten wider, even if I'd ripped her eyelids off. I turned the box off. She continued staring for a few seconds, then she looked at me for the first time in a couple of years. The television silence was new.

"Enough TV, Mom."

"Did your father find you, Josh?"

"Yeah. He punched me, ma. He punched me in the face."

"I'm sorry, Sweetie."

"He ever hit you?"

"Of course not. Will you put the television back on, please?"

"Was he like this when you married him?"

Her eyes closed a little bit, and, for a few seconds, I swear, she forgot about the television. She thought and she looked at me, and the fog seemed to burn off her brain.

"Yes, Josh. Your father was always like this." She took a big shot of vodka, and, bang, the fog came rolling back in, and there wasn't no visibility to speak of. "I'll turn the television on myself." There was a commercial for macaroni and cheese, a kid's food.

I only noticed this after I took a shower, and as I was leaving. The apartment wasn't very clean. It was still cleaner than most, but not up to my father's craziness. The dishes were two levels deep in the sink. There were pieces of dirt bigger than pebbles on the floor. The window over the kitchen sink was actually smudged. It didn't make sense. You want stuff like this to add up. But the only time when things like this make sense is after you're dead, when everybody who's ever known you — heard what you've said, seen what you've done — gets together and compares notes. He did that to you, well, he did this to me. You heard him say what? Listen to this. First he cleaned the apartment, then he didn't. Well, he did the same thing back in '79. Same thing? Exactly. And what about the Teddy bear? He gave me one, too. And the monogrammed pen? Ditto. The son of a bitch. Or sweetheart. Or idiot. Or genius. Now it makes sense. All the sense in the world. But it can't make sense to you because you're dead.

I walked by the school, where Jamal and his buddies were playing basketball. And they were playing hard, not stopping every five minutes to sell some dope through the wire fence. There was a cop watching the game, so drugs were out. But sometimes, even when the police weren't around, the boys forgot about the dope and even their egos — "Dunk on you, baby!" — and played some of the best ball in the city.

"Hey Josh, we need a fifth, you want some?"

I didn't care about sweating. Not anymore.

I was one of the smallest guys out there, which meant that I needed to play guard. Not the best arrangement, see, because I was much better playing power forward with a bunch of short players. I didn't have the ball control or speed to be a guard. I was matched up against Clarence, who would go on to be a star player in college and a pro for a year before blowing out his knee and being made an offer, the only one around, to play in Europe, where he probably makes a couple hundred grand and, I hear, is married to an Italian movie star. Caused a scandal, the white and black hookup.

He got by me whenever he wanted to. I think it was as hard for him as sleeping was, and he was known to doze off in class, joining me and a lot of others. On defense, he stole the ball from me three times. I got one basket, a clunker that bounced around the rim for as long as most people wait for trains. It's called an ugly shot, and the boys were laughing because it was the only way I could put points up. Clarence was nice about the way he overwhelmed me.

"How much your father pay you, Josh," the New York Knickerbocker asks.

"Two bucks an hour."

"Hell, that's less than minimum wage."

"I know. He says I'm lucky to be getting anything because I'm helping the family out."

"I probably get $100 every time I dribble the ball."

"That adds up."

"Hell yeah. You ever seen my house?"

"No."

"It's in Jersey. Got three guys mowin' the lawn."

"I've never mowed a lawn."

"Me neither. You gotta come and see my lawn. I got a fountain, too."

"A naked lady?"

"No. Some kind of spitting flower."

Francis watched me play while he was leaning against a red apartment building. He struck up a conversation with the cop. Couldn't shake his love for the grunt on the street. Told the guy the streets are getting tougher. Me, I'm on assignment now. Yeah, Boston. Been there? No? Great town. My case? Missing person. Could be nothin', could be somethin'. You know how it is. We all know. Francis patted the cop's back, out of camaraderie, but the cop didn't like it, backed off, and headed down the street.

Sports hadn't made me feel any better. Now, I wasn't just sad, but a wet, sad pile of shit, walking a city that had a goddamned pooper-scooper law. Something had to pick me up.

It sure wasn't the Mayflower. Gretchen Himmel was the Citizen of the Week, and the picture, in keeping with tradition, showed her at her worst, a close-up of her face, with all the features out of focus except a hairy mole with some blood dripping from its head. I knocked on Jane's door and thought, she must be sneakin' more cigarettes and her lungs must be pissed, because her voice was unusually raspy. "Come on in." Sitting on the chair, eager for visitors, was a one-legged man with no teeth and a pony-tail of silver hair — the type of pirate I'd expected to run the Cape Cod motel. "Well, don't just stand there lettin' the wind blow in." No wind.

"I'm sorry I was looking for someone else."

"Who might that be?"

"Jane."

"Don't know no Jane. You play checkers?"

"Um. Yeah. But I should try to find Jane. This is room 15, right?"

"Sure is. Pull up a seat. I'm black."

"Josh?"

I turned around and saw the administrator, Mr. Dobson, the only guy in the joint who ever wore a suit.

"Yeah?"

"Can I talk to you for a minute?"

"Hey, Dobson! This boy and me were gonna play checkers."

"That'll have to wait, Mr. Hirtanen."

"Damn. I was gonna be black, too. I never lose as black. Last time I was red and Jenkins whupped me."

Once we were in his office, Dobson told me to have a seat. I did. He smoked, and I smoked. He told his secretary through the intercom to hold his calls, and she did.

"This is always very hard."

Her heart had given up on her. I guessed it had exploded. He said it had happened quietly and quickly. I guessed there had been a lot of noise and the suffering had lasted more than a few innings.

"She'd been hurting for a while, you know... We wanted to get in touch with you, but we didn't have your number... She was a very nice woman... She'll be missed... Always had a kind word... She wrote you a note... Let's see if I can find it... Yes, here it is."

Dearest Joshua,

I'm not going to confess any secrets, as some people choose to do in letters such as this. There are no skeletons in the closet, no buried treasure. Nothing like that.

I just wanted you to know how much joy you've brought me. You've made this empty cold place a little warmer, a little brighter. Your visits have been the highlights of these recent years. I would have liked to tell you all of this, but writing has always been easier for me. I feel less self-conscious when I put pen to paper. For this reason, I hope you can forgive the letter, and not think it ghoulish or morbid.

There is only one observation I can make. This isn't sage advice, just common sense from someone who's seen a few countries and met a few people. You need to find something, Josh, an interest of your own. I've pushed books because they've meant so much to me, reading and writing them. But find your own. Once you do that, I think your life will gain the perspective you have been seeking.

As for your father, if he puts a hand to you, do as I always threatened to do to Lyle: kick him in the balls. It's a wonderful trick.

All for now. That's a stupid to way to end a letter like this, but it seems to be what I want to say!

Love,

Jane

P.S. Don't worry about me. Lately I've enjoyed sleeping more than being awake.

While I was reading, Dobson was piling up one-inch tall metal men on top of a black magnetic base. Now that I was done, he combed his mustache. He probably had no idea that this scruffy, 16-year-old with an unglued life would cry. But he did. I did. A loud and violent cry, like the kind that had come from Manny. A lot of it had to have been junk that I'd kept inside, stuffed in a closet, until the closet door finally broke off its hinges. But a lot of it was plain Jane, all Jane, because it was her face that I saw when I covered my face with my hands. Snapshots of her, better than anything the Mayflower photographer could have done. Jane flexing her muscle, smiling, telling me how she'd taught arm wrestling to an African tribe. Jane pretending to hug the walls of a plane that ran out of gas and crashed in a Japanese rice field. Jane squinting, just as she did after getting fitted for glasses by a blind, Indian optician. Jane stroking my hair.

"Gee, I'm sorry. I know it must be terribly hard on you. If there's anything we can do, please don't hesitate to ask."

He was nice enough, but I didn't want to deal with any sort of Dobson. I thanked him and left, and I wouldn't go back to that Mayflower joint no more, no more, no more, no more.

I was wet with tears, and still wet with sweat. Wet all over the place. In addition to not wanting to get any more wet, I didn't want to continue the games with Francis, who'd dozed off standing up against the Mayflower. Like a horse. He fit in with all the other old folks around the entrance. Best camouflage job yet.

"Francis." He didn't stir. "Francis!"

He opened his eyes, looked at me with a sleepiness I took for fondness, then remembered that he was trailing me, possibly for murder, and that he wasn't supposed to be seen.

"Well, oh my, well, Josh, hi, how are ya, imagine that, beautiful day, a little hot, though." And so on.

"Come on, Francis. Let's go for a walk. I'll show you around the city."

I told him about Jane.

"Hey kid, I'm sorry."

He knew what it was like. Worse, he'd had a wife go. Also the heart. She'd known it was coming, too, knew about it for years.

"That's the type of knowledge that'll kill you. Imagine walking around, doing the little things, the big things, in life, knowing that at any moment your heart's going to fail. Doing the dishes, walking the dog, even in bed. Where can you find any confidence? How can you be sure of anything? Leanne held her head high, though, did everything she needed to do. She was proud. Wouldn't have said if she was frightened. But she was strong, too, and I don't think she was frightened. We all have to go sometime, Josh, and Leanne felt God would take her when he wanted to. It didn't matter whether she walked a little more softly or wore gloves to do the dishes, or anything like that. I know you don't

191

believe in the same type of God she did. Hey, but you said you spend more time in St. Patrick's than in temple, right, so maybe there ain't no difference."

We walked by some dealers. "Smoke, smoke," a few of them said. Francis, after he made out what they were saying (at first, he heard "smo, smo"), told them that he was sorry, but he didn't smoke, had to give it up, on Doc's orders, a few years ago, but he remembered how nice it was to breathe the smoke deep into the lungs. The dealers were confused. I pulled Francis to my side and walked away. When we were clear of them — you got to get clear because some of them are hotheads, hotheads with guns — I told Francis they'd offered us drugs.

"Drugs? Those kids? Are they always black?"

"Around here they are, usually, but go downtown, into the village and you'll find some lily whites in the same business."

"Gee, and there was a cop just around the corner. Boy, if I could have been so close to the crimes, my job would have been a lot easier."

"It ain't so simple, Francis. Take one of these boys off the street, and another jumps in to fill the space. Like draining a sink while the tap's on gangbusters."

It helped to be with Francis. He was no Jane, no replacement. But he was another old folk, a guy with a long past who'd lived his best days when the world was mighty different. Old age means getting further and further away from the good times. Unless your life has always sucked. And it hasn't improved. Only now, you have more pains, and more trouble sleeping.

We walked west, toward the park. He knew about the park, remembered it from the sixties, when he'd see pic-

192

tures on the TV of teenagers smoking pot and sitting bare-ass on the ground and some even having sex, like they had no shame. No shame back then. The line between right and wrong got all fuzzy. There was a handout man on 59th Street. A real pro, this Indian guy, tryin' to grow a mustache even though he shouldn't have, 'cause instead of a lot of short bristles he could only grow a few long strands that seemed more like a dog's whiskers than a human's. But he was good. Twirled in the middle of the sidewalk. Hell, he got me, experienced me, even though I was trying to avoid him. And he got Francis in the groin. Francis was shocked. No one had touched him in the groin since Leanne died, God Bless Her Soul. He stopped in the middle of the sidewalk, again screwing up the New York walk and even surprising the handout man, who wasn't used to these pauses.

"Hold your horses, Josh. According to this piece of paper there's a big sale going on at a drug store around here."

"You need anything?"

"I don't know. I guess I always need somethin'. Young man, your store got a deal on ant-acid?"

"Sir?"

"You know, antacid. Calms the stomach."

"Go to the store, sir. They'll tell you."

"'Cause my stomach gets out of control sometimes. Maybe it's the drink. Know what I mean?"

"Yes sir. Go ask them. They can help you. Big store."

I touched Francis's arm and we started walking. He turned back after a few steps and asked the handout man about getting a deal on shampoo, even though he didn't need so much, ha ha. The handout man didn't hear, or didn't want to answer. He was busy groining pedestrians. We passed the store and Francis stopped to look at the products in the window. They were cheaper than on Cape Cod, he said, but if he bought them now he'd have to carry 'em around and you only want to carry around essentials on a hot day. Yup.

There were Frisbees flying everywhere in the Park. One fell by Francis's feet and he picked it up and accidentally threw it in the opposite direction of the kid who was waving for it. The kid gave Francis the finger. Francis practiced the throwing motion a couple of times, just in case. There were some more guys selling pot. "Smoke, smoke." I shook my head to them. That's what you're supposed to do. Francis turned to one of the guys, a scraggly white kid with long hair and a heroin problem, and said, "Don't push me, punk. You got a mother? She know what you're doing?"

I bought him a hot dog, and he ate it in two bites. He liked it so much that he bought himself another. Then he wished he'd bought some ant-acid at that store. His stomach was wondering why he'd come to New York.

"You know what I like about this place, Josh? It's a big open space, see, in the middle of this huge city, and still, it seems like it's got all these layers, one field here, another there, a path here going down, another going up. All these pockets. You walk into a tunnel and when you come out you see something completely new. You ever been to a baseball game?"

"Yeah. I went to Shea once."

"You know when you walk through the tunnel and come out and see the green grass of the field?"

"Yeah."

"That's what this is like. Boy, I love the sight of that field, and the players tossing the ball around just before the game starts."

Manny

The Central Park fields weren't as green as Fenway, the players here weren't as fine-tuned as the Sox, and the ball wasn't so small and thrown so fast that you actually needed skill to hit it, but Francis said it would be fine to sit and watch a few innings. The match-up was the employees of a steak house versus the DA's office. The steak house boys were at bat for the ten minutes we watched — a few innings would have lasted a few hours — and they were putting on a goddamned clinic, hitting the ball on the ground and in the air, in the holes and right at the lawyers, who couldn't handle it because they were afraid. The Beefcakes scored eight runs, and the lawyers, wearing sports goggles instead of regular glasses, got angry with each other. The third baseman, before the ball shot between his legs, told the first baseman to get down on the ball, and the first baseman, failing to get down on a ball that made the score five-nothing, told the pitcher to stop giving the Beefcakes such meaty pitches. That was after the pitcher rolled a ball, about as meaty as a sparrow, over home plate.

Francis said he was used to heartbreak because he was a Red Sox fan. Then he said he was thirsty. I pointed out a hot dog man and all the sodas lined up on the cart. That wouldn't do. Not that kind of thirsty.

I took him out of the Park to a Blarney Stone, one of the City's stock Irish bars, where real drinkers drink, where you not only can get a shot, but a plate of lukewarm brisket.

Drink one. Francis had a whisky. I had a Coke.

"I don't get the sense that there are a lot of neighborhoods in New York."

"There are some. Little Italy, downtown, is a neighborhood. But most are so big, I think they're too big to be called a neighborhood."

"Boston's got neighborhoods."

"I've never been."

"You never been to Boston?"

"No. Cape Cod was my first trip to Massachusetts."

"You got to come back. I'll show you the sights."

"That would be cool."

"Cool. Yeah. Central Park kind of reminds me of Boston."

"You mean the little nooks and crannies?"

"Yeah, like the English muffin."

"How many people live in Boston?"

"Hell, I've never been any good with numbers. What about New York?"

"Something like eight million, I think."

"You live near here?"

"Not too far."

"You want a peanut butter cracker?"

"Sure. Thanks."

"You know New York good, the streets I mean?"

"I know this area real well. I walk around here all the time."

"I got to know my beat in Boston so good that I could walk it with my eyes closed. I knew where the mailboxes were, right, and the lamp posts, and even where the sidewalk was broken up, where I could trip."

"That's neat."

"I think it's good to know a place good."

Drink Two. Francis had a whisky. I had a whisky, because there was this gorilla sitting at the end of the bar, kept looking at my Coke glass and then at me, and shaking his head like he was gonna have to kill me because I was doing the soft drink thing.

"I don't got many friends. The Henrys, particularly Greg. He's a great guy. I got a brother in Florida, but I don't know if you can call him a friend, 'cause he only calls when he needs money. He starts off talkin' about the good ol' days in Boston, to grease me up, see, then he says he needs a few bucks 'cause his bookie's died and the new guy doesn't let him float like before."

"What's he bet on?"

"Dogs. Greyhounds. Not even a real sport. A bunch of pooches chasin' a fake rabbit. You said you didn't like sports much, but you were pretty good at basketball."

"I just don't like watchin'."

"You were good, but that guy you was playing against, he was the real thing."

"I know. He'll play in college."

"College, huh?"

"Yeah."

"Leanne was my best friend, from the day we started seeing each other until she passed away. The cops were my buddies, but Leanne was my friend, get it?"

"Sure."

"Some of the guys would stay out late 'cause they didn't want to go home. Me, I liked going home. I guess that's why my buddies stayed just buddies. What about you, you got friends?"

"Some. Not a lot. Billy's my best friend. Manny's a good friend."

"Seems it."

"Jane was a good friend."

"It's tough, ain't it?"

"I just wish I knew what was gonna happen before it did, so I could have said something to her."

"If you knew, you wouldn't have been able to say shit. You would have been crying all over your shirt."

"Maybe."

"So, what would you have said to her?"

"I don't know. Goodbye?"

"That wouldn't do it, and you know it. Words can't do it. Ain't nothin' you can say that makes death easier, on that person or on you. I've been there."

"Yeah."

"Hey, you got someone else around, not that anybody can replace Jane or nothing."

"Who are you talking about?"

"Me."

"Thanks."

"I could say that, too. You know, it's hard not having kids, when you think you'd be pretty good at it."

Drink three. Whiskies all around.

"Your father's a character."

"He's an asshole."

"Yeah. My dad used to slap me around, but he always kept an open fist, so it wasn't as bad. But your dad licked you good."

"Why'd your father hit you?"

"Every kid I knew had a father who hit 'em. Sometimes it was bad, like what you got. But mostly it was for discipline, to get you to do something. And you learned pretty quick to do it."

"I don't have a discipline problem."

"Then why does your father get all bent out of shape?"

"He's just all fucked up."

"You ever hit him back?"

"Not really."

"You're nearly as big as he his. You can do it, and that'll make him think. You know where to hit him?"

"No."

"Here, get up. Now you pretend to take a swing at me. Okay. Now, I pull my head back and hit you square in the stomach. Like that. It's always better to go for the stomach. When you get the head, it's a sharp pain, but it goes away pretty fast. When you go after the stomach, it's this dull pain, makes you feel sick, and you're not gonna be doing anything for a while. Like getting it in the balls. You try. Okay, okay. Good."

"You hit him pretty hard before."

"That? That was nothing. He fell down easy. You could take him down if you hit him right. What about your mother?"

"What about her?"

"She around?"

"Yes and no."

"I don't get it."

"She drinks too much."

"That's too bad. I seen booze kill a lot of people. The bottle ain't got too many real friends. It pretends a lot, but it doesn't like you."

"What about you?"

"What? Drinking? I'm one of the real friends. The bottle likes me, really likes me."

Drink four. The bartender told us to put our money away. This round was on the house. The gorilla at the end of the bar was nodding. He liked that I'd moved from the syrup to the sauce. Maybe he was grateful about something else, that the bar was solid, and his glass was always right where he left it, and even his elbows were staying put.

"You still think I had something to do with Patrick?"

"Na."

"And Manny?"

"Na. You got to understand, Josh, I've just been doin' my job, and part of that job is checkin' everything out."

"How much do you make on a job, Francis?"

"Nothin' on this one. Just expenses."

"What expenses?"

"Gas."

"Why'd you follow us here, anyway?"

"I just acted on my instincts. When I saw you pull away, I just came after you."

"We saw you following us."

"What? What do you mean?"

"Oh, nothing. Just as we turned down your street, I mean."

"It's a good chance to see New York, too. You know, back when I was on the beat, Boston was bad, but New York had the biggest criminals."

"You miss it, don't you?"

"What, the criminals?"

"The whole scene, the action."

"Sometimes. Sometimes I feel like I was an athlete who broke his ankle or something and it never healed and he couldn't play no more. But he wants to, boy, he can taste it every time he gets up in the morning, and when he tries to walk he hobbles. I just got old. That was my ankle, see, age, and you can't get healed from that."

"It must be hard, leaving something you don't want to leave."

"It's like a fuckin' death."

"What do you think's happened to Patrick?"

"He'll show up. He always does."

"Can I tell you something?"

"Shoot."

"I think Dorothy is a bitch. I know you're her friend, and you're working for her, too, but that's what I think."

"She can come on tough, that's for sure."

"Tough?"

"All right. So she ain't the good witch of the east, or the west, whatever it is."

"Yeah, east."

"She never knew when to stop with Patrick. None of the daughters ever ran away."

My first time drunk in St. Patrick's. It wasn't real bad. The statues weren't coming to life, walking up to me and asking me for a cigarette, but the flames on my favorite candles were blurry and I didn't get as close as I usually did, thinking the fires would grab me. There were others there who'd sipped or gulped from the bottle, and they were sleeping, feet on the kneeler. I was one of them now, but I wasn't tired, and I'd never put my feet up, no matter how far gone I was.

Francis liked the place, said he'd never seen such a big church. It didn't make him believe or anything. No God would have let Leanne die so young. We walked slowly and unevenly — at least I did. Francis was steady — past the South Transept, the Sanctuary, the Liturgical Altar where I'd once imagined Gina, the Blessed Sacrament, the North Transept, and back to the Narthex. We stopped in front of the information desk, and I recognized the woman. She'd finished studying her church statues. She looked at me. Waved me over.

"You know how you were asking me about Jacob the other day?"

"Yes."

"Well, I read up on him."

"Great."

"He was the bad son, and Esau was the good one. Jacob stole Esau's birthright."

"How?"

"By pretending to be Esau when Isaac, the father, was dying. He got Isaac's last blessing, when it should have gone to Esau."

"Thanks."

"It's helpful to keep up on all faiths, I think."

"I agree."

"Have a good day, okay?"

"Okay."

"Are you all right? You look ill."

"I'm fine, thanks."

The Jews were particularly active on 47th Street. A big diamond shipment must have come in. The grandfathers in black robes and the grandsons, in black jackets because they hadn't yet earned the robes, made for a fast-moving sidewalk, but not fast enough for those in a rock-hurry, who hopped off the curb onto the street and beat the cars and delivery trucks.

"Jesus, this is what I imagine Israel to be like. Look at all of 'em. You ever been to Israel?"

"No."

"Don't all Jews want to go there?"

"I don't know. Maybe a lot of them are curious. You ever been to the Vatican?"

"Hell, no."

I escorted Francis through the exchanges, and he made the mistake of stopping at every stall and raising the hopes of every Jew in the neighborhood. He'd ask to see the biggest diamond in the case and the conversation always went the same way.

"For your wife?"

"No."

"Sweetheart?"

"No, I've just never seen a rock that big."

Francis didn't care for books, couldn't remember the last time he read one. Yes, he could. A self-help book that Gregory had given to him after Leanne died. He needed to grieve, the book said. Grieving's okay. Like he needed a book to tell him that. Francis knew Gregory was just trying to help, and sometimes a friend helps by telling the obvious, but in this case, all that book did was prove to Francis that magazines were the only literature he would ever need and that television was the best goddamned invention since the shag rug.

Francis liked the McGraw Rotunda, particularly the Prometheus on the ceiling. Leanne had been an ace artist, would relax with a canvas and a bowl of fruit. She had been the one who saw that Patrick had talent, even as a little kid. When other kids were drawing stick figures, Patrick was doing shadows. I let Francis pick a title out of one of the black title books in the catalogue room. He filled out the piece of paper and handed it to the woman, the same woman I'd seen a week before. He got his number and we walked into the reading room to wait. I told him how the library worked.

"Pneumatic tubes? You mean there are people underground finding your book for you?"

"Yeah, eight floors of stacks."

"Stacks?"

"Bookshelves."

"And they get the book up to you somehow?"

"By dumbwaiter."

"I seen one of those once, at the house on Beacon Hill. Remember I told you about the smoked dame and the Butler, Osborne?"

"Yeah."

"She had one of those dumbwaiters in her room, see, so she could get some food lifted to her from the kitchen a floor below."

The number board flashed. 26. 27. 31.

"They missed me, Josh."

"Don't worry, that sometimes happens." 32. 33. 35.

"Where am I? They forgot about me."

"Just wait, Francis." 37. 38. 29.

"That's me." Francis jumped out of his seat and cut off a young woman who might have read more than my guy but couldn't match his excitement and speed. We sat down at a table.

"So, what'd you get?"

"A book on painting. Better have pictures."

"They're in black and white."

"What a rip-off."

"Hey, it didn't cost you anything."

"I know it, but what the hell's the point of looking at gray oranges?"

"What does the writing say?"

"Who cares. How much can you say about gray oranges, and look at that, a black banana."

After we got into Manny's apartment, Francis looked around and asked where the rest of it was and Manny laughed, said she would schedule an hour during the week when she could show him the other rooms. But I'm getting ahead of myself. Like in bed. Get it? Get it? When I buzzed up to Manny and she got on the intercom, I asked if we could come in and she wondered who "we" were, and I told her Francis was with me. She hesitated before letting us in. I looked at Francis. He nodded. He understood.

"Good to see you, Francis."

"Hi there, Manny."

"Hey, Josh."

"Hey, Manny."

"So, you liking New York, Francis?"

"Quite a town."

"Chasing any criminals?"

"Na."

"He doesn't think we were involved, Manny."

"I told him that from the beginning."

"I was just doing my job."

"Have a seat."

"Thanks."

"You want a drink?"

"Sure."

"Josh?"

"I'm all set."

Manny was still pissed that Francis had ever thought we were behind Patrick Boy's disappearance. The drink helped. She was wearing a summer dress that just covered the mole in her cleavage. New York City couldn't see that mole, but I knew it was there. Sure, for a few seconds I imagined taking Manny by the arms and sliding her dress down. (In a TV movie they'd show a close-up of the floor and the dress falling on it.) But I knew. Manny wouldn't be my first, or second.

Rizzi buzzed, and I was thrilled that he and Francis would be in the same apartment. Too bad he was dressed for the heat, meaning he wasn't wearing an oversized jacket. But the shirt and pants were big enough to fit Francis. Awkward cuffs everywhere. I introduced him to Francis, and, strangely, my boy was quiet and withdrawn. He was polite, shook hands, but didn't slap Rizzi on the back, tell him about the Boston Blue, about his beat, or even that he was on a case right now, might not look like it, but hey, that's part of the business, right?, not looking like you're doing it.

"No word on Mr. Henry, ma'am. No, I haven't been able to locate Patrick Henry." He still loved the name.

"I haven't heard anything either, detective."

"Well, I'm just checkin' in, making sure you know we're still trying."

"Thanks."

"You know, I been reading about Patrick Henry, not yours, but the old one."

"Is that right?"

"Yeah, the professor lent me one of his books. You know Patrick Henry kept his insane wife in his basement. She was gonzo and he just kept her down there."

"Really?"

"Yeah. You know books ain't that bad. Give me liberty or give me death."

"You got it."

"I'm brushing up on the whole seventeenth century."

Francis didn't like him because Francis didn't like detectives, those power-hungry, headline-grabbing dandies who forget what the uniform means when they're allowed to take it off.

Back on the street, as workers walked home, eager to put the sweat-stained shirt in the hamper, and the fresh T-shirt on, Manny told Francis and me what she'd been thinking about all day.

"I'm going back to work, and I'm not going to look any more. I know I can't turn my feelings off, but Jesus Christ, I gotta go on."

She'd called Patrick's apartment, gotten no answer, and would call again, but more and more, she felt he'd split for some reason, and she wasn't going to let his disappearance do a number on her the way it had on that other girl years before. Ellen. Ellen. When Patrick showed up, she wouldn't know what to think. Part of her would be happy. (I guessed forty percent.) Another part would be pissed. (Sixty percent, and it would only grow.) She didn't care if we agreed, but did we understand?

"Josh?"

"Yeah, I understand. I only know the shit he's brought you."

"Francis?"

"Hey, Manny, you gotta do what you gotta do." Sounds cold. But it wasn't. It was the same type of advice that the self-help grieve book had offered to him. Obvious. He meant it, just couldn't wrap it in a sentimental bow.

We walked by the Plaza and the fountain. I didn't say anything. I looked at Manny, and she looked straight ahead. Francis saw the line of limos and said there had to be a lot of movie stars in the Plaza. He didn't bring up Patrick and spinning.

Mrs. Chung was wearing a yellow shirt with a huge, purple flower covering her breasts, and Francis loved the color, might have loved the breasts, too. He was blushing. When a red face blushes, you think there's so much pressure inside that the hair is going to be pushed out.

"You still need shave, Josh."

"I know, Mrs. Chung. How's business?"

"Up and down."

"Maybe people are too hot to eat."

"We have air conditioning."

"That's true. I brought two friends to eat your wonderful food."

"Good. I give you round of drinks free."

"You don't have to do that."

"I know. My restaurant. Go sit down."

Mrs. Chung's other son — not David — was on duty, and he took us to a booth. There was an old woman sitting at my table, using chopsticks to pick vegetables from the serving dish. This Chung was an engineering student, but I didn't know him well. And he was too busy studying all the time to know me as a regular and to have in his head, along with theorems about pulleys and bridges, the chow mein I always ordered.

Manny used two saucers of duck sauce to cover the assorted appetizers. Francis said he'd seen a guy wolf down two pints of fried clams for dinner, but he'd never seen so much duck sauce on one plate.

We could have had our after-dinner drinks in the Oak Bar, and I could have stuck with a Coke, but Francis had a taste for the seamy side, far from the money, and I was ready to go at it again, now that my stomach was calmed by chow mein. The place Francis chose was named "Bar". One pool table with felt that, where it wasn't torn by a drunken shot, was worn white. Small wood tables with gray, knit tablecloths that sucked up spilt beer so well that you wouldn't need a napkin. If you needed a napkin for some other reason — say, if you'd had a few, and had eaten the bowl of pretzel nuggets and wondered why you were still hungry and someone told you the nuggets, now broken up, hadn't made it to your stomach because they were hanging on your beard — there was a fan of them in the middle of the table.

It was our good luck. Whisky night. A shot for a dollar.

Francis handed the bartender a twenty. Told him to keep 'em coming. The guy didn't like that. Said he'd run a tab, and we'd pay when we were done.

There were only a few people in there with us.

Francis asked Manny about her life, boyfriends and stuff. He wasn't fishing anymore. She told him about the ad business, her parents, the assholes she'd been with. She said things had seemed fine with Patrick, but don't things always seem fine until, bam, you pull the curtain, and there it is. Now, she was going to try to live without the curtain. She'd been independent since she was a kid, did things her own way, but she always felt she needed someone, thought she couldn't be whole without a guy.

"You guys ever been happy alone?"

"Speaking for myself, Manny, things haven't been the same without Leanne."

"What about you, Josh?"

"I don't know."

"I guess I'm just beginning to see that alone doesn't have to be bad."

There were two seedy guys sitting at the bar, smaller than gorillas, bigger than me. They could have been plotting a heist, see, arranged this meeting to draw up the plans, talk about timing, down to seconds, memorize the layout of the place, make sure the job would go perfect. Made me think of Francis and the riffraff he'd seen and fought and missed.

"Who was Joey the Mouth, Francis?" He took a belt and slammed the glass on the table. He squinted. Got quiet. Looked around. He was back in history.

"Why do you bring up the Lip?"

"Just curious."

210

Oh, the Lip, one of Boston's best. Died like a little man, disease of the gut, lying on a prison bed, but before that, when he was operating on the outside, he was a prize, a cop's fuckin' dream. The name? Guy could talk anybody into anything. He'd offer you a buck for your left arm and you'd cut it off and forget about the buck. Wasn't handsome or nothing, had this pug nose and a big, hairy mole on his cheek. But he always knew what to say. The ladies loved him, 'cause tough guys don't always know when to change gear, the difference between a job and a date, but the Mouth knew, told 'em how beautiful their eyes were and how their dresses made those curves mighty irresistible. And he was the same in his dirty businesses. Sweet-talked people into deals that helped him, hurt them, and they didn't realize until it was all over. And it's not like they were bitter. No sir. They'd just laugh at themselves for falling for a bad deal, and they'd say the Mouth was a talent, good thing he wasn't a cop. He's one of those guys that people love to please, cut off an arm just to see a smile on his face. 'Course, it didn't last. Never does. Even the best opera singer loses her voice after a few years, see. He couldn't do his magic on this young thug who was thinkin' big and who set him up for us. We got Joey. And his sweet talk didn't help him in the joint, where people's ears ain't open the same way as on the outside. When he died, he was just like everybody else. We all look the same when we die and when we go to the bathroom. Can't hide nothin'.

While Francis was talking, the two seedy guys were drinking up whisky night, and getting louder. One had a long beard that he would have to shave to accommodate the ski mask. The other was clean-shaven and had greasy flat hair that was perfect for the head wrap. Francis and Manny chatted — could have been about the Mouth or Patrick — and I watched the riffraff. I heard a laugh with an evil twang, and the bad guys stood up, walked over to us. They didn't ask to sit down, just pulled up a couple of chairs around Manny. We ignored them for a couple of seconds. Francis knew creeps. I did, too. Manny knew the most.

"What can we do for you, guys?"

"You hear that, John?"

"Oh, yeah. She asked what she do for us."

"Come on, guys, give us a break."

"Did she say come?"

"Oh, yeah. She did."

The bearded one put his hand on Manny's shoulder.

"Hey! Buzz off creep." She pulled the hand off.

"Don't get upset now, baby."

"The lady said to scat." Francis's hands were fidgeting on the table.

"Watch your blood pressure, grandpa."

"Listen, punk. I'm telling you to go. If you don't, you're in trouble."

The greasy-haired one, John, touched Manny's ear with his dirty finger, and she stood up.

"You got soft skin."

She turned and punched John in the face, in the left cheek, and he fell back a few steps. It was a good punch, but these guys were drunk, couldn't feel pain normally. The bearded one grabbed Manny from behind, around the waist, and spun with her in his arms, five or six turns, before she was able to kick his shin and make him let go. He laughed. Then Francis, big Francis, pushed the table over and slammed the bearded one against the wall, my boy's hand around the bad guy's throat. The beard tried to talk, but the sound

212

wouldn't come. He tried to grab Francis, but the hands wouldn't reach.

"I told you to go, punk."

John walked by me and punched Francis in the back of the head, a funny place to hit him. Francis let go and the beard struck a huge punch to the belly. Francis bent over. Manny kicked John in the back of the leg.

Where was I? Didn't I do something?

I walked behind John and tapped him on the shoulder. Could have been asking him for a light. Could have told him he had a call. Could have told him his car was waiting. I gave him the Francis cut to the stomach, as hard as I could, and he fell to the painted wood floor coughing and struggling to breathe. A second later. Francis did the same with the bearded one. It must have been a bigger hit because the guy fell, and he was silent. It didn't take long, though, for him to start coughing. Manny tried to kick both of them in the balls. It was a difficult kick because they were all bunched up. She didn't connect with the bearded one. But she hit John squarely and he cried like his daddy had just told him that, no, you ain't getting a skateboard, not today, not tomorrow, not ever.

Francis leaned over them.

"I warned you, punks."

Manny.

"We warned you. Assholes."

Me.

"You ain't got nothing on us, see. If I ever come across you again in this city, and I'm everywhere, man, I'll fuckin' break your legs. Got it? Got it?"

I stepped on John and I stepped on the beard. I threw the bartender one of Genius Uncle Saul's twenties. It landed on the floor, and I wasn't about to pick it up for him.

It was raining outside, and we ran across the street to stand under an awning. There were a lot of people standing there with us. New York City had left the umbrellas at home.

Even though Francis was puffing more than he probably ever did after collaring hoodlums in Boston, he was smiling like a kid who finally had been given that skateboard. Manny asked if he'd been hurt.

"Me? I feel great. You okay?"

"Yeah, I'm fine. Thanks for your help."

"You didn't need much. You're a tough lady. I like that."

"It would have been different if you hadn't been there."

"You handle yourself real good, Manny. You're all right."

"You, too, Francis. You're all right, too."

I'd never felt happier hearing two people talk. Manny said she was going home. She was tired. I asked Francis if he wanted to do something, maybe catch a movie. No, he was going to hit the road. He was done in New York. Gert needed him.

Manny kissed Francis goodbye. I shook his hand, and as I did so he put his free hand on my shoulder. It was as close to a hug as we could get.

"We'll be in touch." The last thing he said to us.

7

After Francis hit the road to Cape Cod, and after Manny hit the streets to the upper west side, I went to Billy's. The next morning I called the city. Asked if I could get a divorce from my parents. I made some clerk's day, made her laugh on the job like she hadn't laughed anywhere in years. I asked about changing families, somehow. Paperwork, she said. Paperwork. She'd be happy to hook me up with a case worker. I didn't want a case worker.

I split my week between Billy's house and mine. It was hard at first, being with Mommy and Daddy, because Daddy still liked to whack my head. But that ended two months into the school year. The Francis-taught stomach punch to my father didn't make life the greatest thing since the shag rug, but it got the asshole off my back. I was standing in the apartment, pouring some orange juice for breakfast, when my father walked up behind me and stopped to watch, making me nervous, so I spilled some on the counter. He slapped my head, and I spilled some more. I put the juice carton down, turned, and gave him a fine chop to the stomach. He fell to the ground, like he'd done in Francis's driveway. I told him never to touch me again. I cleaned up the orange juice and sat down next to my mother, who was singing along with the Cookie Monster on Sesame Street.

I didn't feel bad seeing him on the ground. I was empty, except for the slightest sense that it was right, him being there, and me being where I was.

My father stood up and thought about coming after me, but he backed down, stormed out of the place, slammed the door, dislodged the top nail of the mezuza.

My thoughts haven't changed much, so many years later. Maybe I'm angrier. That David Lipkin could slap around a pretty nice kid and that the kid would feel nothing, except the slightest sense of rightness, in finally hitting Daddy back.

My father never touched me again. He cursed when he wanted to give a whack, so there was a lot more cursing in the place, but that didn't bother me at all. I worried that he'd take it out on my mother, but he never did, at least when I was around, and she didn't show any signs of getting beaten up during their intimate moments alone, if they had any. My mom stopped getting dressed and doing her hair. Every time I see a nightgown, even on my wife — thank God she prefers nude to nightgowns — I think of my mother, and the thoughts aren't good.

I had sex with Gina in November 1983. 'Course, I'd done it before. Wasn't like I was a virgin or anything. Yes, I'd done it before. Gina said Laurie had told her about it. It'd been quick, sure, most first times are, but I'd been sweet, embarrassed, yes, but not an asshole, not the kind of guy who gets mad at the girl, says she did something wrong, when, if anything, she did something right. Laurie said so. One of life's little mysteries solved. The little ones get solved.

Manny finished her guitar and named it Walter. She was proud of it and had always liked the name Walter, and why shouldn't objects have names? It's not as though they don't have personalities. There wasn't any glue showing on Walter, and she'd made a beautiful green, yellow, and red mosaic inlay around his sound hole. The best part was his neck, with Mother of Fucking Pearl designs in each fret. She learned how to play a few chords, and we'd sing "Blowing in the Wind" a lot. She had a cocktail party once, and one of the guests was a guitar player, and he said Walter was among the best he'd ever picked.

She dated off and on for the rest of the time I knew her, but it was never anything serious. She said she was going to try to adopt a baby on her own. She'd not met a man who would do, and she wasn't holding her breath. Of course it would be nice to have a guy, but life could be rich without a bunch of men's underwear all over the place, without another toothbrush in the bathroom, without someone stealing the sheets from you in the middle of the night, without the mind games and disappearing acts.

Billy went off to Yale. Hated New Haven but loved the math. After graduation, I worked for a year at Genius Uncle Saul's lab, making copies, delivering packages, helping out with experiments when Saul thought my interest in life and the lab was heading south. On cold days he let me eat my lunch in the hot room, where they grew bacteria, and on hot days I dined in the cold room, where I could put my can of Coke on dry ice.

Yes, I went to college, City College. Did so well that my academic advisor only had to ask me twice if I felt school was the right choice for me just then. My wife was an English major. We took Introduction to the Modern Novel together. But we talked for the first time when we ran into each other outside of class, in a coffee shop in the village. Hey, aren't you in Professor Lerner's class? Yeah, hi. Hi. Hi. Now, whenever I see someone get off the bus or get into a cab, I don't think that I'll never see 'em again. I know it's just a matter of time before I see that lady, that guy, that kid. I'm gonna meet a lot of people in this life.

Patrick? He never showed up.

In 1988, I was walking with Manny on the subway platform at the 72nd Street stop. We're at the same underground depth as busy gophers racing to find books for folks in the Reading Room. The downtown train pulls in. One crowd gets off and another, including us, gets on. We're holding onto our straps, but before the doors shut, we hear, "Hi Manny." She turns towards the voice, toward the closing doors. She puts her hands on the window, and her breath fogs up the glass. I look over Manny's shoulder at the people walking away from us. I see their briefcases and purses, the good posture and bad, the mohair coats and woolen business suits, and the backs of the heads. Brown hair. Black. Hats. The fancy kind with leather straps, the useful kind you pull down over your ears, and blond hair.

Manny turns back to me. There's a pregnant Hispanic woman holding the hand of a toddler. There's a bum with a hand outstretched and his eyes closed. The train is dirty, smells, makes a lot of noise. Manny stares at me for a second, and I expect her to say something big. She asks if the movie starts at 7:35 or 7:45. I tell her. 7:35. But it's Bergman. It's not like we're going to be less confused if we miss a few minutes. Hell, we could just watch the credits and be as plugged in as anyone. Or not go at all and write a goddamned dissertation on it. Get an "A".

Mother Mann and Barkface got married in 1989. Manny never warmed up to him. Couldn't stand a guy whose face was as rough as her papa's hands and who had taken her papa's place in bed, the bed that papa built.

In this world, every year, there are more births than deaths. I must be living somewhere else.

Manny got sick. She called and told me the news, and I went over and I cried and pretended to be strong, cried and pretended some more. She didn't cry. The way a flame eats every match in a matchbook, that was cancer in the Mann family. The doctors tried a lot of techniques, but nothing worked, and it took them six months before they said the most important thing was to make her comfortable. I'd visit her at Mother Mann's apartment three times a week, then two, then one. It was overwhelming to see her, the body I had wanted, and the voice that had been so big, everything gone, like the bubbles in a bottle of Coke left open. She understood why I couldn't come, and when I was there, she wanted me to go, because she knew what it was doing to me. And I was in no position to help her. I was a selfish asshole. Couldn't see her pain through mine.

I walked the streets, trying to call up images of Manny — person and body — as I'd known her. I want to see her eating a hot dog. Cheering the '86 Mets. Pouring duck sauce on her appetizers. Waltzing with me at her brother's wedding. Mopping up after Squeaky. I want to hear her saying "shit" and "fuck" and "hell, even monkeys know how to masturbate." But all I see is a shell, a voice that moans, a smile that says don't worry, the pain isn't all that bad, or thank God it can't last.

Hers was the first untimely death in my life. Every other one made sense. They hurt, but I could understand them. My mother was relatively young, I guess. But she did it to herself, didn't she? I'm not gonna say I didn't cry when Mom went bye bye. I soaked my goddamned pillow. But it's not like I wanted her to stick around, so we could have more of the same, so she could go on sticking a funnel in her mouth and pouring the vodka in, and I could keep trying to see through the brain fog, only to crash on the fuckin' rocks. No way.

The difference with Manny is that I did want more of the same. For the few months after, the hardest part was that she wasn't available, to call or bounce an idea off. I'd get something going in my head and the first thing I'd want to do is tell Manny, my friend. I called a few times, got a message from the recorded operator. The number had been disconnected. When I got over that, and it took several months, if I found myself laughing at a joke, I'd slip back into a thought about Manny. Or if I was spacing out, staring at a vacuum cord, with my head as empty of thought as possible, Manny's death bed would call me back for another visit. It got easier. Soon, the first thought rushing to fill my empty head would have nothing to do with Manny. At that point, if I wanted to think of her, I could, without being overwhelmed, teary but not flooded.

Then it took a bum turn. The distance from her death should have lightened my heart, and it did a little, but it also lightened my head, which made the heart thing worse. I was forgetting what she looked like. Sure, I had some snapshots, and even without them I could picture her still life. But her movement, her life, was fading. Her hand couldn't wave. Her head couldn't nod. Her eyes couldn't blink and, if she was sad, the tears couldn't leap. When I closed my eyes and tried to remember standing next to her while she was hailing a cab, it was me standing next to a cardboard cut-out with a prop-guy behind it, pulling a string or flicking a switch that makes the fake hailing motion work. I once slept next to her, and her butt didn't feel like cardboard.

Now I can see her move. It just takes time. Resurrection.

I see her when I read the paper, when I see those boxed-in pictures of kids up for adoption, smiling sincerely because they're happy despite things or forcing a smile because life sucks and smiles don't come naturally. I see Manny in the background, hugging the kid, rocking from one side to the next, whispering into a little ear a joke that only they know, that only they share. A good mother.

Our last real conversation, before she stopped answering, before she stopped opening her eyes, before she stopped.

"Hi, Manny."

"Josh."

"How are you, Manny?" I needed to say her name. Manny. Manny. Shit.

"Not too good."

"Can I do anything for you."

"Kill me."

"What?"

"You heard me, Josh."

"Don't think like that. You're gonna be fine."

"Can I have some water?"

"Sure. Here."

"Is Squeaky here?"

"No, she's not."

"I miss Squeaky. Squeaky girl, here girl."

I leaned over her, got as close to her face as I'd ever been. Her eyes were more often closed than open, and when they were open they darted around quickly. Like she was just being born, taking it all in for the first time.

I put my mouth to her ear. It tickled her. She shifted her head. I inhaled. Through the odor of hair that hadn't been washed, and through the stink of disease, I smelled her.

"You know something?" She didn't answer. I sat up. Her eyes were closed. "You know something?" Her eyes opened and flew around the room. When I put my hands on her cheeks, her eyes stopped on me.

I leaned over again and whispered.

"You're so strong. You are so strong, Manny."

For a few long moments I looked away, at the wall. My hands gripped the bedspread, stained from someone having spent too much time under it. My lips trembled. But when I turned to her, I forced them into a tight smile. She was still looking at me. Her eyes were calm, at rest. She lifted her right hand. I folded it around my face. It was cold and wet.

222

It was weak. But I wanted it touching me.

Manny nodded. She smiled. God, I couldn't imagine her pain. But, at least for a little while, I had seen beneath the smile and beneath the pain. I could now see her clearly.

"You are so strong." But I just mouthed the words. Nothing now needed to be said, for either of us.

One day the doc tells Francis to ease up on the drinking and Francis tells him to blow it out his ear, because drinking is a quality-of-life issue and neither a doctor nor a preacher has any business in that department.

1994. He was down to one or two investigations a year, and they were all small-time. This rich dame couldn't find her dog. The police were no help and the dog-pound people called her irresponsible for letting the dog out of the house and off the leash. Didn't she know there was an animal population problem on Cape Cod, and in the whole fuckin' United States? First thing Francis did was call the dog-pound people and tell 'em that if they ever talked to the dame like that again he'd come in and spring the locked-up spaniels and shepherds, and make the animal population problem a whole lot worse.

Gregory's version goes like this. Francis is driving around a neighborhood he doesn't know that well, not wearing a seat belt, because they're for folks who live in fear. He's borrowed four articles of clothing from the dame — a bra, two blouses, and a skirt. Couldn't bring himself to ask for panties, even though they would have been best, because he's trying to get her scent. Makes sure she hasn't washed any of it. He drapes the stuff on his car, keeps it in place by rolling up the four windows and catching some ends inside.

And he's driving, hoping the dog will smell the old lady and come to him, assuming that the dog wasn't trying to get away from that smell in the first place. Francis is probably down because after all those years tracking down Joey the Mouth and Righty he's looking for a dog and got an old lady's wardrobe hanging off his Chevy. He's got a bottle of whisky with him and he's holding nothing back.

Some teenagers out joy-riding pull up alongside him and start laughing and pointing fingers. Francis can't hear what they're saying because his windows are rolled up and he doesn't want to roll 'em down and lose a bra or blouse. The kids pull away, and Francis is either pissed off big-time or convinced they have something to do with the missing dog. Maybe he sees a shadow in the back seat and thinks it's the dog. It's not, just a kid's pony tail. So Francis chases them, and they speed up. And we got a drama shaping up on the quiet streets of Cape Cod. The kids are thrilled, won't let themselves be caught by an old timer with a bra waving from the driver's side window. And Francis, for a few minutes, is back in the world of bad guys and good guys, when bad guys had good names, and he takes a few belts and won't let up on the accelerator until he gets his man or men. But my boy's reflexes are bad. Age and booze. A truck turns the corner and my boy forgets where the brake is and he turns off the road, crashes into an oak tree that's been around as long as he has. Acorns cover the Chevy. Inside, all over the seats and floor, there's a stew of whisky and peanut butter crackers. Francis lies next to the tree, the whisky smell on his mouth, an acorn resting perfectly on his forehead.

He died faster than he was born, and he once told me his mother spewed him out faster than a loose crap.

Francis, when I think about you these days I break out in a big smile, and there are no regrets. None. Wherever you are, we gave you another story to tell. You're talking about Manny the same way you used to talk about Joey the Mouth and Righty. I can hear you.

"There was this dame, see, and she was tall, legs up to here, and damned if I didn't think she'd done it to the guy, killed him, used a gun or a knife or poison and slipped the body under some New York City floorboard. Murder. You got it. She pretended to be soft, sure, but I'd put my time in and I knew soft from sandpaper. She was sandpaper, see, the coarse grain. Her black sweater might have been soft, like her brown and black dog, the bitty-bladder runt she called Squeaky. But not her. Like I said, the coarse grain. I'd seen it all before. A million times. Maybe more."

Tiffany Elizabeth Mann.

Francis, truth is for a while I thought she might've done it, too. You never knew this about me. Yeah, I pictured her pummeling Patrick with a cast-iron bench plane and slipping him under some rickety floorboard. But I fell in love with her, Francis. I got to know the gentle lady. She wouldn't throw a log into the fire before making sure there weren't any bugs on it. Did you know that? She could identify all the snaps and pops of a fire, and would cringe and say "Shit" when she heard a bug explode. Now I do the same thing with my logs and my fires and my bugs. Shit. My wife thinks I'm not over her. That Manny isn't over for me, and what I've said about her hasn't been a "closure."

Got a baby. Boy. Francis Lipkin. My wife fought the name a little. I said it would do wonders for the Irish-Jewish dialogue. She said she'd never heard of an Irish-Jewish dialogue. It's big, I said. Bridging the gap between Gaelic and Yiddish. *Paug mahone*, schmuck. It means, kiss my ass, schmuck. If the kid had been a girl, I would have wanted to name her Manny, and my wife would have fought more.

I carry Francis on my shoulders and he pulls my hair and eats it. He likes it almost as much as his peanut butter crackers. I have the day off, see, and we're doing the New York Walking Thing. The old lady's reading in the library.

Francis tosses some pebbles into the water at Grand Army Plaza and he's thrilled by the ripples. He laughs when an employee at FAO Schwarz throws him a red, inflated ball that bounces off his head and disappears into the air. He doesn't like St. Patrick's, a dark place. He's frightened by the information-desk woman, even though she's caved in and bought dentures.

The streets are smoking, a warm day after a night of cold rain. When we walk down 47th Street, Francis sees all the Jews and their robes and jackets, and he yells "black, black, black." It's a good thing we're not in Harlem. A nice man at the library lets Francis stick the canister with my book order into the pneumatic tube, but my boy cries because he doesn't want to see his little arm taken underground.

Manny

Francis's expression changes when he sees Mommy behind a stack of books. I leave him with her, I kiss her soft cheek, and I go up to the number board. 22. 24. 25. 26. 28. This is mine. This is my book, Francis. This is my book, Jane. And Manny, it's your book, too. I'm gonna read it to my son in the Reading Room.